2

E-BOY

ANH DO

E-BOY

2

ROBOFIGHT

Illustrations by Chris Wahl

ALLEN&UNWIN
SYDNEY • MELBOURNE • AUCKLAND • LONDON

First published by Allen & Unwin in 2021

Allen & Unwin
83 Alexander Street
Crows Nest NSW 2065
Australia
Phone: (61 2) 8425 0100
Email: info@allenandunwin.com
Web: www.allenandunwin.com

A catalogue record for this book is available from the National Library of Australia

ISBN 978 1 76087 785 9

For teaching resources, explore www.allenandunwin.com/resources/for-teachers

Cover design by Jo Hunt and Chris Wahl
Text design by Jo Hunt
Set in 13/22 pt Legacy Serif by Jo Hunt

Printed and bound in Australia by McPherson's Printing Group

10 9 8 7 6 5 4 3 2 1

The paper in this book is FSC® certified.
FSC® promotes environmentally responsible, socially beneficial and economically viable management of the world's forests.

CHAPTER 1

'Come, one and all, to the Robofight Games!'

President Bonner shouted into the microphone with all the gusto his short, round frame could produce. Thousands of people in the arena cheered and threw their hands in the air.

Bonner smiled. *All these cheering idiots*, he thought. *No wonder I could fool them enough to become president!*

He continued. 'Look at these amazing pieces of robo-science! Over the next week, we'll see them battle until only one remains.'

Bonner motioned to six awesome-looking robots in the middle of the arena. Well, five awesome-looking robots and one that looked like a big metal soccer ball.

No distance weapons were allowed in Robofight – no missiles, bullets or beams – which resulted in a frightening array of blades, clubs and even the occasional tentacle glinting in the sunlight.

The tournament favourite was Harkland's entrant, Arachnatron. Arachnatron was a two-metre-tall spider. Each of its eight legs was lined with razor-sharp barbs and ended with a heavy hammer.

Where a real spider would have mandibles at its mouth, Arachnatron had two titanium-tipped drills.

The robo-beast reared up and the crowd cheered, the Harkland supporters cheering the loudest.

Each of the six robots stood on a round platform, while an eighth platform was empty. Bonner gestured towards it. 'Our head technician apologises for the transport issues that have prevented our own Titus entrant being part of today's ceremony.' There were boos and jeers from the crowd, but Bonner forced his smile to stay in place. 'Once again I say welcome, and good luck!'

Bonner strode off the podium and grabbed an assistant by the elbow. 'Has the lab communicated anything? Is it ready?'

'Y-yes and no,' the assistant stammered. 'I mean, yes, we've heard from the lab, and no, it's not quite–'

Bonner snorted and stormed off.

'No. Not here,' said Penny.

'Why not?' Ethan pouted. 'We deserve a bit of luxury – we've travelled almost three thousand miles in three days!'

They'd taken buses and trains between small towns and walked when they had to, trying to avoid major cities and their surveillance cameras.

Ethan had monitored the police networks for reports, so they knew if they had to change clothes, or avoid certain roads.

At night they would slip into any motel that had electronic locks on the doors and find a vacant room. Sleep didn't come easy.

Less than a week earlier, Ethan had gone from teenage brain-tumour patient to superhuman with the power to hack any – *every* – electonic system by thought alone.

Penny had gone from world-renowned surgeon and roboticist to fugitive, and her greatest creation, Gemini, had gone from soulless android healer to assassin.

Ethan and Penny's heads were spinning.

Now, they stood at the main entrance of Lloyd Towers, the most luxurious hotel in the city.

'We have to keep a low profile,' Penny insisted. 'We have to be average in everything we do, including where we stay . . . President Bonner will probably be staying here, with all of his security! We want to be close, to try to find out what he's up to, but not that close.'

Ethan didn't answer. It annoyed him that she was right.

Penny gave a sympathetic smile. This had to be tough on someone Ethan's age. 'What's nearby that isn't quite so flashy?'

Ethan closed his eyes, and spread his mind through travel websites. As he searched, it was like looking at a roadmap of the city with every street drawn in shimmering silver. Hotels, motels, and anywhere offering a bed was a coloured dot on the map – and the colour was almost always red, for No Vacancy.

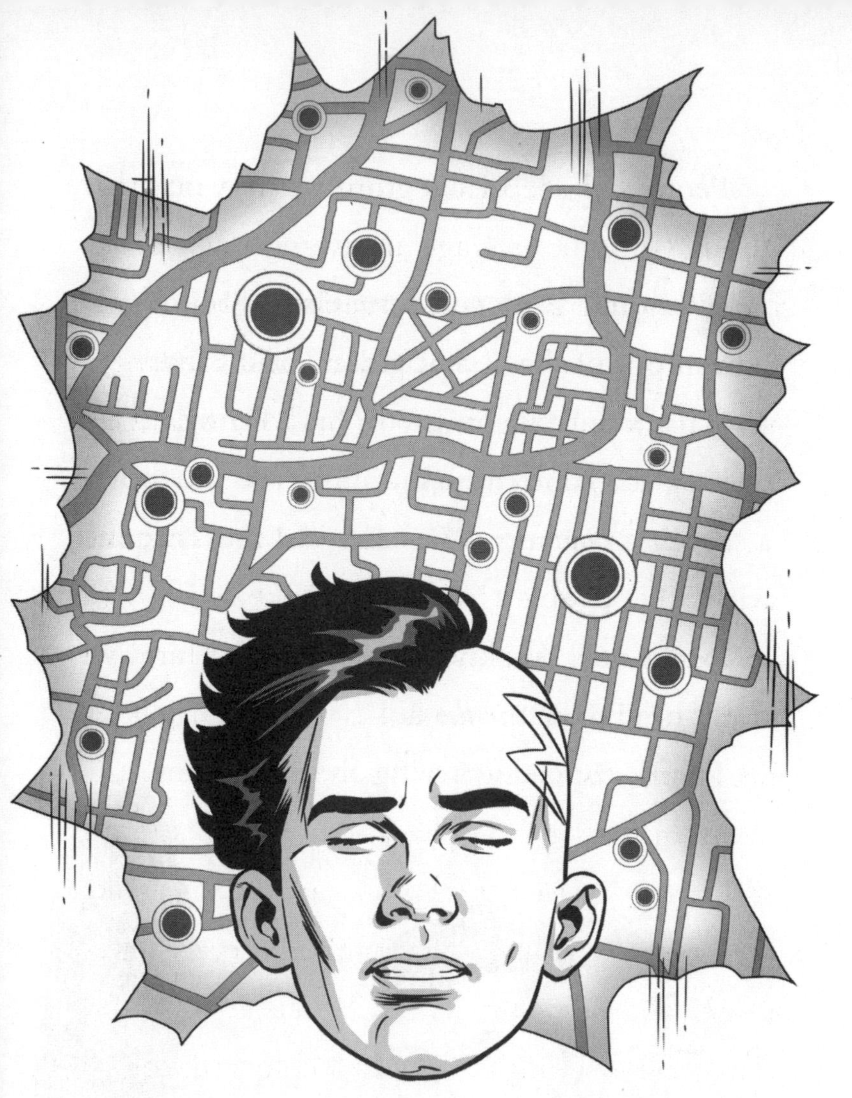

'Everything is booked out. It's the Robofight Games. Only the dingiest places in town have anything left.'

Penny sighed. 'Well, I guess we have no other choice.'

'We could swap someone else's booking for ours at one of the decent places,' said Ethan.

'That's not fair on them,' said Penny, trying to keep her tone from sounding too much like a scolding teacher's. 'We can't just mess around with other people's lives. We'll make do.'

'Make do?! You know how powerful I am! We don't need to just *make* do!'

Penny stopped worrying about her tone.

'Ethan, every time we take something that isn't ours, someone else suffers. Yes, you're powerful, and that's a lot to deal with, but that doesn't give you the right to take whatever you want. The whole reason we're here is because powerful people are doing what they have no right to. We're trying to stop them, so we can bring your parents home and get our lives back, not be *like* them.'

Ethan didn't reply. Penny couldn't tell if she'd gotten through. Then her phone beeped as an email confirming a booking at the Kwikstay Motel arrived.

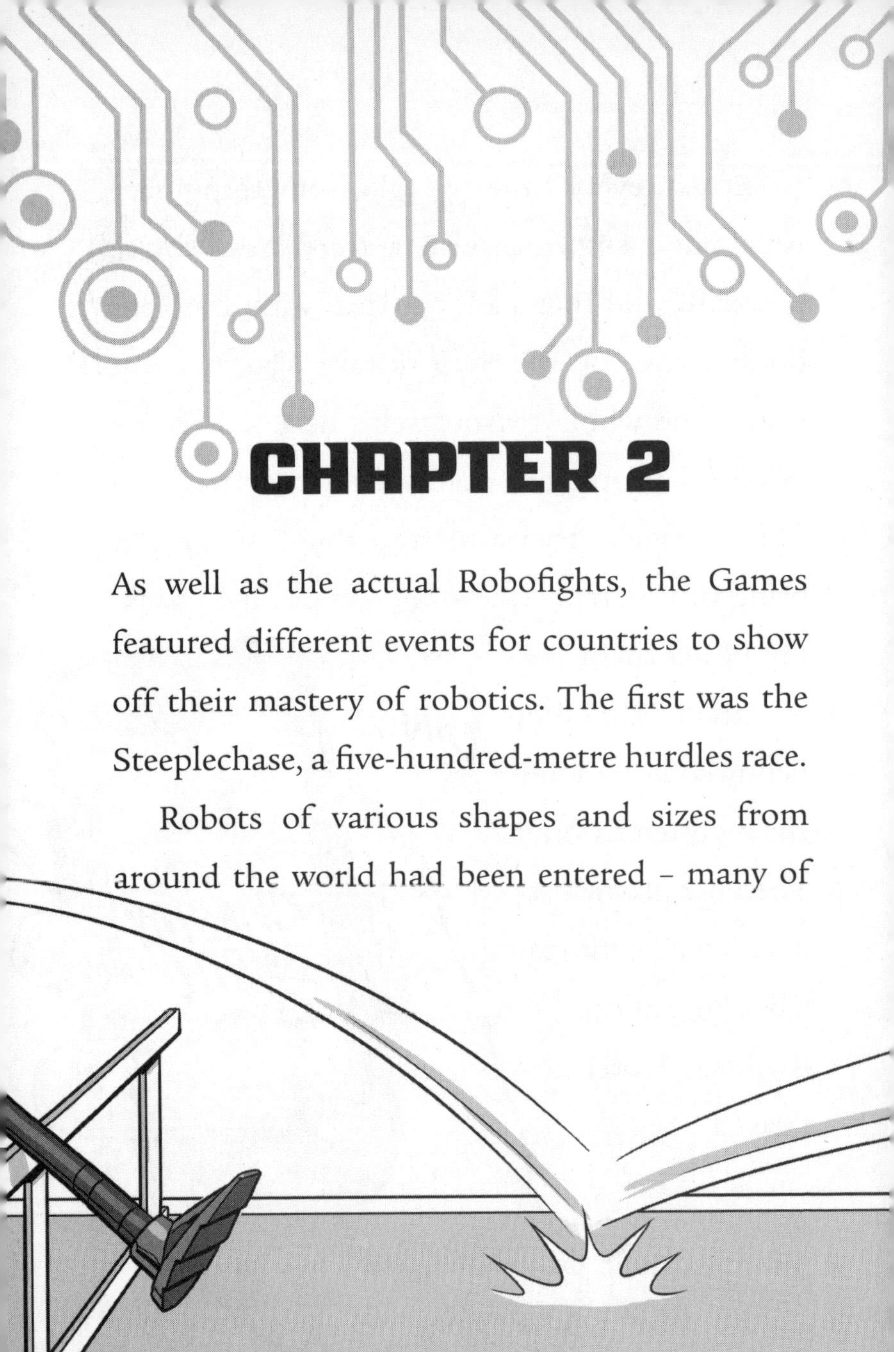

CHAPTER 2

As well as the actual Robofights, the Games featured different events for countries to show off their mastery of robotics. The first was the Steeplechase, a five-hundred-metre hurdles race.

Robots of various shapes and sizes from around the world had been entered – many of

them were trying to imitate horses or other animals. But the winner, from Japan, was a simple X-shape that cartwheeled along the track.

Just as the race finished, Ethan and Penny made their way into the standing-room section above the expensive arena-side seats. From where he stood, Ethan could see the windows of the boxes just below the stadium's roofline. He could see the back of a TV camera in one. *That's probably the President*, he thought. He looked up at the Channel 8 helicopter hovering over the arena.

Ethan's thoughts reached to the camera. Through the lens, he saw a pale, thin man, hair as black as his long coat. He was looking at a striking red-haired woman who was holding a microphone and talking. Ethan concentrated a little harder to hear what she was saying.

'. . . first visit to this country and his first visit to the Robofight Games, the North Kingdom's enigmatic leader, William James. Mr James, welcome.'

'Thank you,' William replied, his voice chilling.

'The North Kingdom has never entered the Robofight Games. Are you here because that's about to change?'

William smiled. 'Perhaps. I've been invited to the Games each time, and thought it would be interesting to finally attend.'

'Well,' said the presenter, 'we certainly hope you enjoy the Games.' She turned to the camera. 'The first bout is ready to start, so it's back to the studio.'

The signal from the camera went dead. Ethan's thoughts snapped back into his own head as trumpets sounded around the arena.

RF
RF
RF

Huge red curtains parted at each end of the battlefield. At one end, a two-metre-tall cylinder scooted in on shielded wheels. Five sawblades wrapped around its exterior, spinning in an uneven pattern, threatening to shred anything that they touched. On top of the cylinder were six long metal tentacles.

A voice boomed from the arena speakers. 'The first entrant in this opening contest represents the Nations of the Arid Plains. This is . . . Nightmare!'

That name fits, thought Ethan. *That thing is terrifying!*

From the opposite end of the battlefield the oversized soccer ball rolled in, its surface smooth except for the outlines of hexagons and pentagons covering it.

'The second entrant represents France. This is . . . Battle Moon!'

Both robots made their way to the centre of the arena, stopping on marks ten metres apart.

'At the sound of the horn, the contest will commence,' said the announcer. 'Good luck . . . aaaaand FIGHT!'

The horn sounded, and immediately a pentagon on Battle Moon's surface snapped open and a spike shot out, punching a hole in the base of one of Nightmare's tentacles.

It retracted just as quickly, the gap in Battle Moon's surface closing in a blink. Battle Moon rolled backwards out of Nightmare's reach as the damaged tentacle slumped against the cylinder's side, and was immediately cut off by the spinning sawblades.

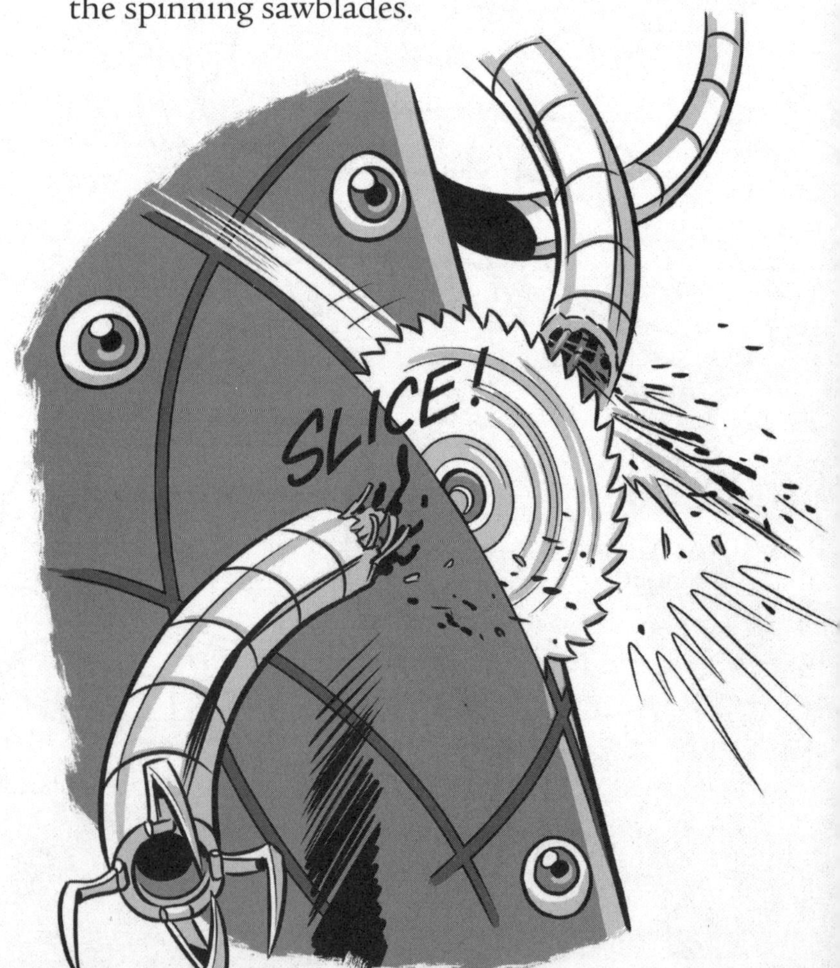

Nightmare closed in, but the tentacles could not find anything to grab on Battle Moon's surface. Battle Moon rolled to the side and another spike shot out, stabbing between the rotating blades and disappearing again. Nightmare kept approaching but its tentacles couldn't catch hold of anything, and each time one of Battle Moon's spikes tore a hole in Nightmare.

The screens around the arena showed reaction shots from the crowd.

Nightmare approached again, but this time when Battle Moon fired a spike out, one of Nightmare's tentacles grabbed it. Battle Moon tried to reel it back in, but Nightmare's grip was too strong. Out shot another spike, and another tentacle wrapped around it.

The crowd could hear Battle Moon's gears grinding as it tried to retract its spikes while Nightmare started to pull them wide, slowly bringing Battle Moon closer and closer to the sawblades.

Sparks flew as the blades scratched into Battle Moon's surface. The crowd watched on in a hush. Suddenly another spike shot out of Battle

Moon, through a sawblade and into Nightmare. A motor in Nightmare gave a growling noise as it tried to keep spinning the stuck blade, but the spike stayed firm. Both robots shook, as the teams of technicians monitoring each of them watched them overheat.

There was a loud BANG, a shower of sparks, and thick smoke rose from Nightmare as its tentacles slumped.

Battle Moon pulled its spikes back and rolled away as Nightmare twitched, wobbled, and then fell with a thunderous CRASH.

'The winner of the first contest,' shouted the announcer, 'is BATTLE MOON!'

The crowd cheered as Battle Moon rolled back to its curtain. Members of Nightmare's technical team drove a forklift onto the arena to carry the robot away.

Ethan stood with his mouth open, then said, 'That was *amazing!*'

Penny frowned. 'Seems like such a waste to me, to see two incredible pieces of technology do that to each other,' she said. 'But let's get on with why we're here. Can you find President Bonner?'

Ethan closed his eyes. 'I can look through all the TV cameras to find him.'

'His VIP box probably won't have any,' Penny said. 'He'll want some privacy away from the media . . . what about security cameras?'

Ethan looked around and spotted a camera nearby. 'Let's see what I can do.'

CHAPTER 3

Ethan walked up to the closed-circuit camera and reached out, with his hand and his mind. He found the feeds from the VIP boxes and searched from one to the next. All he could see were the rich and famous, sipping champagne and mingling.

After a few attempts, he looked into a room with four men inside. Three of them were in black suits – Ethan recognised Agent Ferris, and there were two other People's Service Agents. The fourth man was President Bonner, talking to Ferris.

Ethan could see the President's lips moving but couldn't hear anything. *I guess this security camera doesn't have a microphone*, he thought. *The President likes having secrets.* Bonner looked annoyed.

Ethan pulled his thoughts back just enough to see the flow of information along the camera network and pinpoint which box Bonner was in. He returned to his body and found Penny standing beside him.

'He's up in that one,' Ethan said, pointing to a VIP box about eighty metres away.

Penny led him into the stand, along a grey concrete corridor, up a set of stairs, slowing as they saw two agents standing guard. A beep sounded, and one of them grabbed a device from his hip to study the screen.

'President is on the move,' the agent said to his partner.

Penny and Ethan glanced at each other. Ethan looked up and found another security camera, sending his thoughts through it back to the President's VIP box, just in time to see the door close as everyone left.

Ethan rode the data stream to the next camera and watched the President and his agents walking to an elevator. Agent Ferris slid a keycard into the slot beside the elevator door, which slid open, and all four men entered.

Ethan whispered to Penny, 'I saw where they went. We need to get past these guys.'

'We can't let any agents see us,' said Penny. 'What can we do?'

Ethan focused on the agent, and the device he'd received the message on. His mind reached into its circuitry. The device beeped.

The agent picked it off his belt. 'The President wants us in his box, making sure it stays secure while he's gone.'

Ethan's plan worked, as both agents left their post to move off in the direction of the VIP box. Ethan and Penny snuck around the corner to the elevator.

'I don't suppose we need a keycard,' said Penny.

Ethan just smiled as the door opened.

The elevator took them down. And down. And down, deep underground.

After what seemed like forever, the elevator opened to reveal a bright metal corridor. At the far end was a gleaming steel door. Ethan looked around, with his eyes and his powers, for any security cameras or other devices, but found nothing. He and Penny walked to the door and found a simple lock – one that needed a key, not a card, to open.

Ethan pointed to the lock. 'That's a problem. I can't do anything with that.'

‘Can you feel what’s on the other side?’ asked Penny.

Ethan closed his eyes. After a moment he placed his hand on the door. He stood silent as Penny held her breath.

‘What can you see, Ethan?’

‘Nothing. No networks, no circuits, nothing.’ Ethan opened his eyes. ‘What . . . what do we do?’

On the other side of the door was a long staircase carved from the rock underneath the stadium.

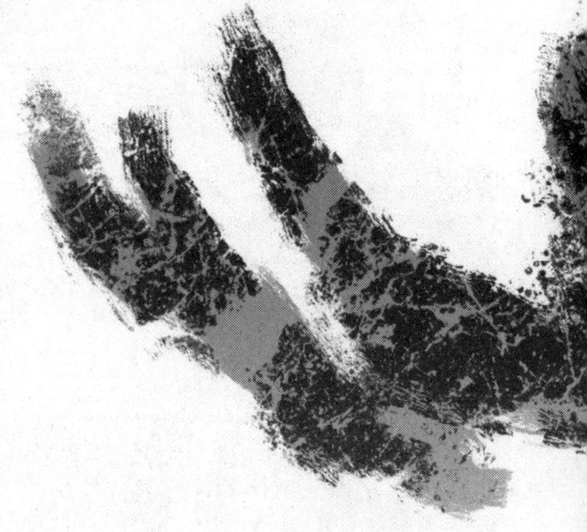

At the bottom was another metal door with a traditional key lock. Past the door was a long room containing a tonne of lab equipment, being operated by four technicians working as hard as they could. There were also three agents, and one president who was puffing and panting.

'Do we . . . *puff* . . . have to keep this . . . *wheeze* . . . so far down?' said Bonner.

'This hacker is amazing – we have to keep this place isolated,' said Agent Ferris. 'No systems running in or out.'

'But I have to go back up all those stairs!' said Bonner.

'What about us? We have to go up and down them several times a day,' said one of the technicians, Doctor Jakoby Ross, who was just as portly as the President.

'Then stay down here and work! We need this thing ready,' snapped Bonner. He pointed to the workbench in the centre of the room. Lying on the workbench was Gemini.

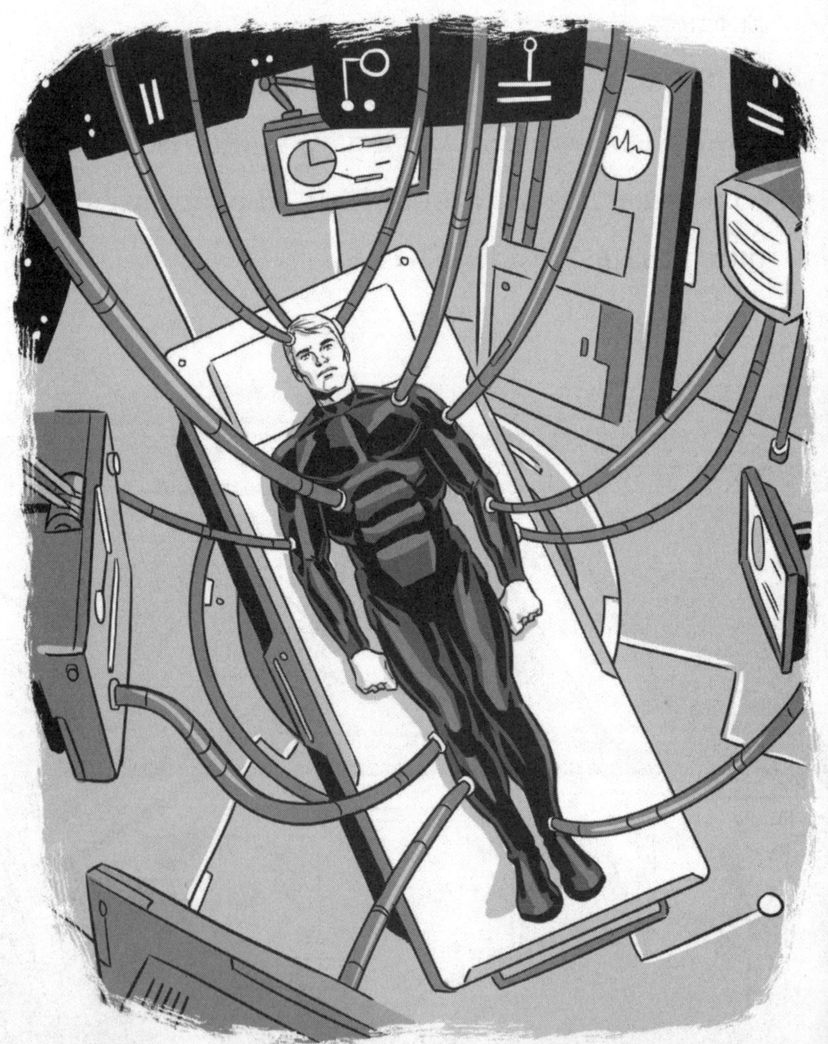

'We're close,' said Ross. 'Whatever happened in that car factory left Gemini in pieces. His hardware is working again, but his systems were scrambled. Part of the problem was using him as an assassin when his core programming was to heal people, but adding programs to fight other robots doesn't clash. Of course a fight with a robot designed for nothing but combat will do more damage to a revolutionary–'

'I get it, Doctor Ross,' Bonner interrupted. 'You don't approve. You don't have to approve to do your job. Will it be ready for tomorrow?'

'We're uploading more combat styles now,' said Ross. 'There's a command that keeps popping up and slowing the process down, but that's probably just a side-effect from the damage.'

'I have to get back to the box for the next bout,' said Bonner. He sighed at the thought of climbing all those stairs. 'Get it done.'

As Ferris unlocked the door, Bonner had one more question. 'What's the command that's getting in the way?'

'*Terminate E-Boy*. Whatever that means,' said Ross.

CHAPTER 4

Ethan and Penny took the elevator back up into the stands, without saying a word.

As they stepped out, Penny said, 'We'll just have to keep watching Bonner. They must have spent a lot of money and effort to make a secret place here. We need to work out why.'

Ethan stood, frowning.

'What's wrong?' Penny asked.

Ethan shook his head. 'I was just getting used to being able to go anywhere, do anything . . .'

Penny put a hand on his shoulder. 'Everyone has limits,' she said. 'Even E-Boy. And even President Bonner. We'll figure it out.'

Ethan's heart beat faster. 'I . . . uh . . . you go back to our spot in the stands. I need to check something.' Penny's expression changed to concern, but Ethan said, 'Don't worry. I'll be there soon.'

Penny squeezed his shoulder, then turned and headed for the stands. Ethan reached into the security system for the elevator and found the logs, deleting the ride he and Penny had taken. He looked up at a security camera and rode along its data pathway, erasing any sign of his presence from the video files, then set up a loop so that anyone looking would see an empty corridor instead of any of his movements.

He heard a *ding* from the secure elevator, and ducked behind a column as Bonner and the agents came out. Ethan watched as they passed him, and saw a silver flare in an agent's pocket.

Only one of them has his phone on, he thought.

Ethan sent his powers back into the security system and removed the video loop, then returned to his spot in the crowd beside Penny.

'I'll be able to hear Bonner from now on,' he told her.

'The next fight is about to begin,' Penny replied. 'You concentrate on Bonner, I'll watch the arena.'

'Yes, boss,' said Ethan.

Penny gave him a wry smile as the trumpets sounded.

The red curtains parted, and from one end came a vaguely human-shaped robot. It stood almost two metres tall, with four arms instead of two. It had no hands – two arms ended in razor-sharp shears, the other two in flat, square blades like shovel heads.

'Looks like the world's angriest gardener!' said Ethan.

Penny laughed. 'Shouldn't you be watching the President?'

The announcer's voice echoed around the arena. 'The first entrant in this contest represents Oceania. This is . . . the Gardener!'

As one, the crowd burst out laughing.

'The second entrant represents Harkland,' said the announcer. 'This is . . . Arachnatron!'

Cheers erupted around the battlefield as the enormous robot spider came from the other end. The ground shook with each step of its sledgehammer-like feet. Arachnatron loomed over the Gardener, the drills in its mandibles whirring.

'At the sound of the horn, the contest will commence,' said the announcer. 'Good luck – and begin!'

Arachnatron raised a hammer and brought it down, hitting . . . nothing. The Gardener cartwheeled out of the way and lashed out with his shovel arm. A jet of oil shot from one of Arachnatron's legs, which shook.

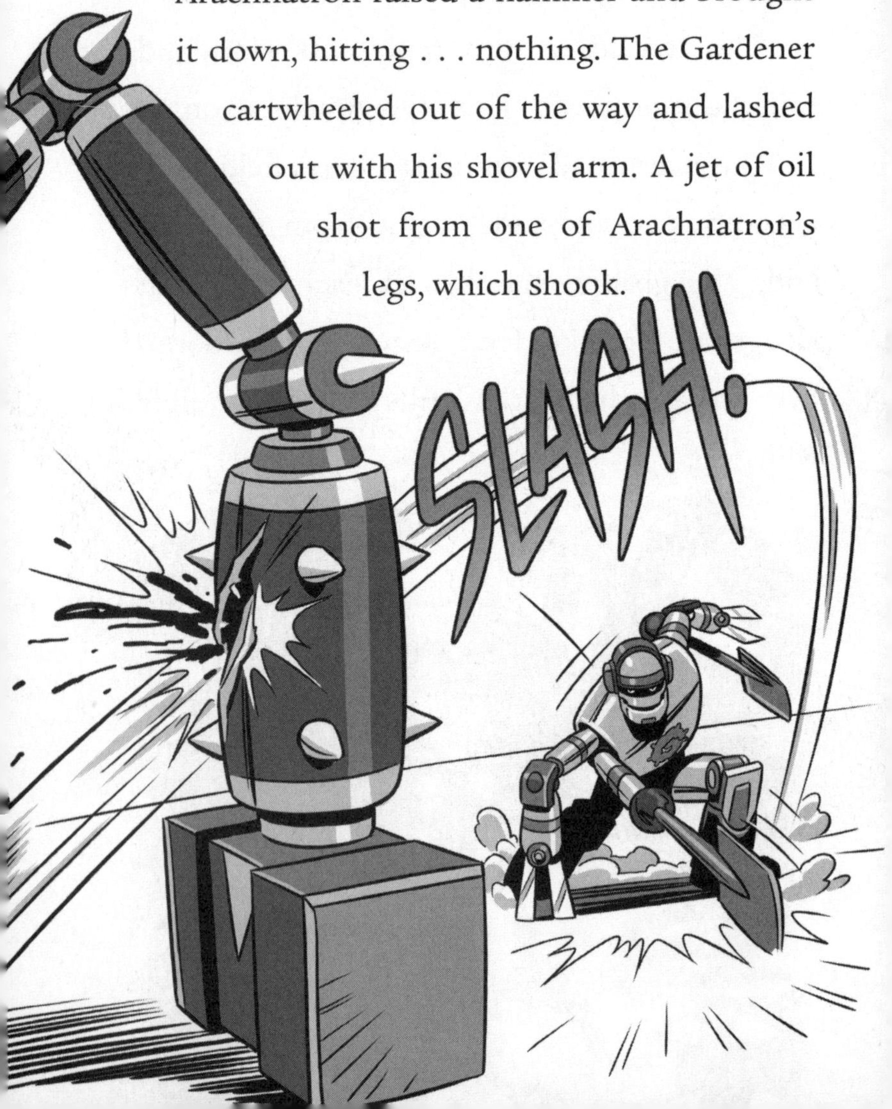

SLASH!

Arachnatron kicked back with another leg. The Gardener dodged the hammer, but the barbs along the leg scraped against its chest, sending sparks flying.

Arachnatron swooped in with another leg to follow up, but the Gardener raised its shears. There was the sound of tearing metal and one of Arachnatron's hammers fell to the ground,

Both robots retreated, checking to see how much damage they had taken.

The crowd sat quiet, then cheered as the robots closed in for another round. Ethan grabbed Penny's sleeve in excitement.

'Ethan, focus,' said Penny.

'Bonner and the agents are busy watching. I'll spy on them again once this is over, I promise,' said Ethan.

Arachnatron sent blow after blow at the Gardener. The Gardener dodged one to the left, another to the right, but the third ploughed straight into it and sent it onto its back. In a blink, Arachnatron followed up with two hammers side-by-side but hit nothing except dirt as the Gardener rolled out of the way.

THUD!

The Gardener approached, swinging a shovel down, then shears up, shovel down, shears up. Tiny scraps of metal flew off Arachnatron with each hit until the Gardener tried one downward thrust too many.

Arachnatron pinned a shovel to the ground, bending it, then trapped the Gardener's head between two barbed legs. The section of the crowd from Harkland cheered louder as Arachnatron brought its mandibles to the Gardener's head.

With a metallic whine, the titanium-tipped drills went in either side and pierced the armour plating, wrecking the Gardener's processing unit. In an instant Arachnatron's mandibles and legs pulled back, and its opponent crashed to the dirt.

A few watchers from Oceania threw their hands up in disappointment, while the rest of the crowd exploded in cheers. Each robot's tech team came out with a forklift to retrieve their combatant.

Ethan tapped back into the agent's phone but couldn't hear anything. He switched to the box's security camera, and saw that Bonner and the agents were all still. Clearly the last fight had left an impression. Bonner turned to Agent Ferris and started talking, so Ethan swapped back to the phone.

'. . . back to the hotel,' Bonner said. 'And tell Ross to work harder.'

'Ethan? Ethan?' Penny's voice dragged Ethan back to his body.

'What's going on? Is something wrong?'

'Your nose. It's bleeding,' said Penny.

Ethan's head had also started to ache. 'I was swapping between networks really quickly. I didn't realise how much effort it takes.'

Penny handed him a tissue. 'Did you hear anything?'

'The President's headed back to the hotel. Should we try that door again?'

'Are you okay? Have you had nosebleeds before?' asked Penny.

'Yes I'm okay, no it hasn't happened before, and before you ask, yes I'm sure I'm okay,' Ethan replied, dabbing his nose. 'I'll check to see if the coast is clear.'

‘You should bring your helmet tomorrow, it will make things easier,’ said Penny.

‘And make me look like a spare robot,’ said Ethan. ‘Now shush for a minute.’

He returned his mind to the cameras. The VIP box was empty, and the two agents standing guard near the VIP section were gone. A camera in one of the carparks showed the crowd being held out of the way so that the presidential motorcade could make it through.

‘I think we’re good,’ he said.

CHAPTER 5

Ethan and Penny edged their way carefully back to the elevator. A few minutes later they were back at the door with the simple non-electronic lock.

'So we're back here, and I still don't know what to do,' said Ethan, frowning.

'Maybe I do,' Penny said. 'I'm used to different mechanisms.' She drew a hairclip out of her hair.

'I used one of these to open padlocks when I was a teenager. You're sure the agents are gone?'

Ethan closed his eyes and focused his mind. 'There are none near the elevator or the VIP section, anyway. There are a few normal security guards around.'

Penny bit her lip, then knelt down at the lock and slid the hairclip in.

Her eyes narrowed as she tried to feel the inside of the lock. After a long moment, she felt something move. She twisted further, and an ear-splitting alarm rang through the corridor.

Penny jumped up and looked around. Ethan was frozen in place, so she grabbed his wrist and pulled him back to the elevator.

Penny had to shout to be heard above the alarm. '*Can you get the door open?*'

Ethan clenched his eyes shut. 'I CAN'T CONCENTRATE! IT'S TOO LOUD!'

Penny tried hard not to panic. 'YOU HAVE TO TRY HARDER!'

Ethan felt blood trickling from his nose, but managed to push the feeling and the noise away until the door opened. Penny dragged him into the elevator and Ethan managed to get it moving.

The noise grew quieter as the elevator rose, but as they returned to ground level there came the *WOOP WOOP WOOP* of another alarm sounding. Penny hauled Ethan to a nearby bathroom, and Ethan tapped into the alarm system and shut it down.

Penny sat Ethan on a toilet and grabbed a fistful of toilet paper. 'What happened there?' she asked as she wet the toilet paper under a tap.

'There were no chips, nothing computerised. I would've felt it,' said Ethan as Penny used the wet paper to clean the blood from his upper lip.

'I must've completed an electrical circuit with the hairclip,' said Penny. 'That set the alarm off. A simple circuit with no computerisation. They're starting to figure you out. That was awful. Such noise.'

Ethan's head was clearing. 'We got out,' he said. 'We're okay. Let's get out of here.'

Penny poked her head out of the bathroom just in time to be spotted by a security guard. 'HEY!' he shouted.

Ethan still felt weak, but had enough energy to run, using his power to turn lights off behind them.

They bolted as fast as they could along the corridor, footsteps and shouting still behind them. They passed two doors that said *AUTHORISED PERSONNEL ONLY* and kept sprinting. The third door had no sign on it and Ethan dashed through it, running headfirst into a mop.

'Ethan, this is a cleaner's closet!' said Penny.

'Get in, quick!' Ethan closed the door softly after them.

A few seconds later they heard the footsteps stop outside the door, and saw a flicker of torchlight underneath it. Ethan and Penny held their breath, then Ethan remembered what he was doing. He resumed turning lights off further along the corridor, and the guard, thinking they were still running up ahead, took off again.

Penny eventually got up her nerve to peek out. Nothing. They crept back out to the corridor and found that the next door after the cleaner's closet was an emergency exit.

As Penny drove them back to the hotel, Ethan said, 'I'm going to find the blueprints for the arena online tonight. We can't get stuck like that again!'

Penny gave a small laugh, but Ethan could see that she was still shaken. 'You did good in there,' she said to Ethan.

'You too,' he muttered back.

In that moment he came up with an idea. Two, actually.

Once back in his room, Ethan spent a few minutes on his computer, surfing the web without typing, before he went to bed.

CHAPTER 6

The next morning, Ethan knocked on Penny's door. She was brushing her teeth as she answered.

'What are you smiling about?' she asked.

'I had an idea about how to wear my helmet at the arena without it being too obvious. Listen to this.' Ethan turned on the radio without touching it.

Penny looked suspicious.

The DJ's voice cut in over the last few notes of a song. *'And remember, if you're heading in to the Robofight Games today, we're giving a prize for the best robot costume out in the crowd. Remember, nothing actually sharp or pointy, but apart from that, go wild with those outfits! It's coming up to news time—'*

The radio snapped off. Ethan grinned.

Penny returned his smile. 'How did you manage that?'

'I went through the radio station's emails, found one about the Games, and snuck it in. Straight away, three people were fighting over who should take credit for the idea!'

Penny nodded. 'That was really clever. And now you can avoid those nosebleeds, and wear your helmet in plain sight,' she said, her smile getting wider.

Ethan could imagine that smile getting wider still when his second idea arrived.

There was a knock, and Penny jumped.

'It's okay,' Ethan said. 'Open the door.'

Penny did. Outside was a delivery man carrying the biggest bunch of flowers she had ever seen.

'I thought you looked a bit spooked yesterday, well I was spooked too, I guess, and it's all been pretty nuts, and I just thought I could do something nice, and I hope you like flowers, well doesn't every girl like flowers? Not that you're a girl, I mean, you're a woman,' blurted Ethan, the words spraying from him like a broken fire hose.

When Penny turned around she was frowning, and Ethan stopped.

'Ethan. How did you pay for these?'

The smile vanished from Ethan's face.

Penny spoke quietly. 'Ethan, I told you we couldn't just use your powers to take what we want. That bunch of flowers looks expensive, which means there's a florist that's going to be out a lot of money–'

'I just wanted to do something nice.' Ethan rushed for the door. 'I'm going to have a shower . . .'

Penny said, 'Wait . . . look, it was a lovely–'

The door slammed.

'–idea . . .'

CHAPTER 7

Additional subroutines added. Combat styles enhanced – hardware repaired. Extra mass on body – armour plating attached %sadg081257terminate E-Boy4asfb$#ppog(Sensory equipment functional.

Reboot complete.

Gemini opened his eyes.

'Hello, Gemini,' said Doctor Ross. 'How do you feel?'

Gemini looked around at the cables connecting him to various pieces of equipment. 'My systems seem to be operational, Doctor. Some memory logs appear to be damaged. May I ask where we are?'

Doctor Ross paused, then said, 'Curious.'

'My GPS is not pinpointing a location. Either it is malfunctioning or we are some distance underground. I would like . . . it would help my systems check,' Gemini continued.

'We are well below the Robofight arena,' said Ross.

Gemini looked blankly at a wall, then said, 'My internal records do not include the term Robofight, and I am currently unable to access the internet.'

Ross held up a USB stick and inserted it into one of the machines attached to Gemini.

Gemini was still for a few seconds. 'Thank you, Doctor,' he said. 'I deduce that I have been given the extra combat software because I am an entrant in the Robofight Games. Is this correct?'

Ross said, 'It is. Does this worry you?'

'I am government property,' Gemini said, 'and do as I am instructed by those who have authorisation.' *Even if those instructions may do me harm.* Gemini wasn't sure where that extra thought came from.

'Are you ready?' asked Ross.

'Unless there are more updates, further delay will not make me more prepared.'

Ross's eyes narrowed. *That almost sounded irritated.* He thought of the staircase from the lab to the arena and sighed, then had an idea. *This will test if he's irritable.*

'Gemini?' said Ross.

'Yes, Doctor?'

'Carry me up the staircase.'

Gemini didn't hesitate. 'Do you prefer piggyback or over the shoulder?'

CHAPTER 8

In a sea of robot costumes, Ethan stood in the arena stands in his E-Boy helmet.

The first battle of the day was over – victory went to a robot that reminded Ethan of a charging hedgehog.

With his helmet, Ethan had been able to switch from watching the VIP box's security camera to listening through the agent's phone easily, and without any nosebleeds. Bonner and the agents hadn't done anything interesting, which was good for Ethan because he didn't want to talk to Penny right now.

Penny said, 'We can't stand here in silence all day, Ethan.'

'I'm concentrating,' he replied.

The trumpets sounded, the curtains parted, and in rolled one of the competitors. Its bottom section was caterpillar tracks like a tank, and its top was a tall column topped with three jackhammers on swivels.

'The first entrant in this final Round

One contest represents Equatoria. This is . . . Hammerhead!'

There was a smattering of applause, but most people in the crowd were saving themselves for what was to come.

'The final entrant in Round One represents . . . Titus!'

A huge cheer shook the arena. People jumped up and down, flags were waved – a few people even saluted.

Red smoke started to pour in from the open curtain as the clapping went from general applause to a steady rhythm, willing their champion to step out.

'THIS . . . IS . . . GEMINIIIIII!'

The cheering grew even louder as Gemini strode onto the battlefield. He was clad in black armour with red stripes, and wore a simple black

helmet with the visor up. Two huge swords were strapped to his back in an X-shape. Gemini looked at the crowd as he stepped up to the red line, then brought the visor down.

Ethan looked at Penny, who wasn't moving. She said something he couldn't hear.

'I didn't catch that,' said Ethan.

Penny had no expression on her face. 'Gemini was in that room. The one we couldn't get into.'

Gemini stood at the red line, facing three sharp jackhammer blades.

Subroutine: swordflourish001

He drew his swords and spun them rapidly all around, bringing more cheers from the crowd.

Gemini stopped, and looked at the swords. *That was not my decision. Inefficient use of battery reserves. Deleting subroutines named swordflourish—*

The horn to start the battle sounded, and a jackhammer blade crashed into the visor of Gemini's helmet, knocking him onto his back.

Helmet dented, vision reduced to less than half.

Gemini flicked the helmet off just in time to see another jackhammer about to connect. He rolled sideways, avoiding strike after strike that thudded into the ground. Swords still in hand, Gemini pushed his fists into the ground and vaulted to his feet.

Identifying vulnerabilities.

Hammerhead's casing was a single metal sheet moulded around its frame – no gaps to slide a sword into. The jackhammers, though, needed gaps to be able to move. In an instant, Gemini calculated angles and strategies.

Hammerhead closed in. The first jackhammer jabbed straight forward, the second arced around in a semicircle, the third made another jab. Gemini dodged each blow, gathering information.

The jackhammers lashed out again, this time with the arcing strike first, then the jab, then the arc. Gemini continued to evade the blows.

Each time, Gemini would take a few steps back, and Hammerhead would close in with a combination of attacks. Jab, arc, jab. Arc, jab, arc.

Confirmed. First and third strikes in each sequence identical.

The crowd grew restless as Gemini dodged but didn't attack. Gemini took a few extra steps backwards and then stood ready.

Hammerhead moved in and jabbed. Gemini dodged the jab, but stepped into the arcing strike. The tip of the jackhammer sliced through the armour plates at Gemini's waist, cutting into his side. The hit caused some damage, but it left Gemini in the perfect position to plunge both swords into the base of one of the jackhammers.

The blades slid deep into Hammerhead's central column. Gripping the hilts of his swords, Gemini stretched into a handstand, putting every ounce of his weight into the blades as they slid deeper into Hammerhead. Sparks and oil flew into Gemini's face, reducing his field of vision.

Hammerhead thrashed and spun, like a rodeo horse trying to buck off its rider. One of the jackhammers hit Gemini on his side, sending him flying.

Hammerhead kept thrashing but started to slow, gears grinding to a halt. It stood unmoving for a moment, then crashed to its side. Cheers filled the arena as the crowd started to chant.

'TI-TUS!!

'TI-TUS!

'TI-TUS!'

Subroutine: victoryflourish001

Gemini stretched his arms out wide and spun the swords like propellers, then clashed them together over his head. As he raised his arms, the slash in his side opened further, sending a streak of oil down his leg.

Those flourishes have to go.

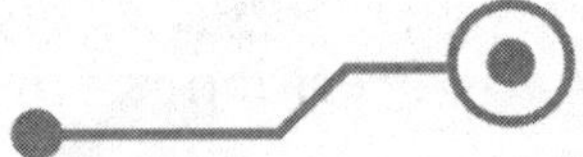

In the middle of the cheering crowd, Ethan and Penny stood still. Ethan sent his concentration to the VIP box and saw an extra person standing there, a roundish man in a white lab coat. While Bonner had a big smile on his face, the man in the lab coat looked unhappy. As Bonner went to speak, Ethan flipped over to the agent's phone.

'—did well, Doctor Ross. You should be proud.' It was the President's voice.

'I still don't see why we're risking such a valuable, innovative piece of equipment as Gemini in this destructive event.' *That has to be the guy in the lab coat*, thought Ethan.

'Doctor, this is bigger than you know. We need Gemini to beat Arachnatron in the final, because Titus needs to go to war with Harkland. Harkland is making new and terrifying weapons to invade neighbouring countries, but they're not ready yet. If Gemini wins over their robot, our people will have the confidence to back a war with Harkland, and we can stop them being a threat.'

Silence, then Bonner started talking again. 'Fix our boy up for the next round, Doctor Ross.'

Ethan heard a door close. He was just about to switch back to the security camera when he heard Agent Ferris speak. 'Why not tell him the real reason?' Ferris said it lightly, like he was telling a joke.

'That I need a war,' said Bonner, 'to distract everyone from the election? To make myself more popular? I don't think Ross would approve.'

Ethan brought his thoughts back to his body and saw Penny had a strange look on her face.

'What's going on?' he asked.

'I'm just getting really sick of seeing the healer I made used as a weapon,' Penny said.

'It gets worse,' said Ethan. 'President Bonner wants Gemini to win so he can start a war.'

Penny looked confused, then said, 'We really need to get inside that room.'

Ethan shook his head. 'I've been looking through the cameras – there are a lot more security guards after yesterday's alarm. More agents, too. We're gonna have to find another way.'

Penny's shoulders slumped. 'There might not be one.'

CHAPTER 9

On the workbench in the underground lab, Gemini lay stripped of his extra armour. A technician was busy reconnecting damaged circuits in Gemini's side with a soldering iron.

Doctor Ross looked at a screen as information about Gemini flowed across it. 'How was the fight, Gemini?' he asked.

'Successful. The armour reduced my speed, but this did not prevent victory. The flourish subroutines are proving unhelpful. I would be more efficient if they were deleted.'

'It's called playing to the crowd, and it serves a broader purpose. Unhelpful or not, they stay,' Ross replied.

Ross focused on the screen. *Gemini's oil circulation sped up when the blade cut its side, but its processing slowed down by a few nanoseconds.* 'Gemini,' he said, 'what happened when Hammerhead damaged you?'

'Mobility in that side reduced by one-sixth, made worse after I . . . *played to the crowd.* If you were to remove that subroutine–'

Doctor Ross frowned. 'Are you trying to . . . insist?'

Gemini stopped talking. The readout showed the same surge in oil and drop in processing speed. Doctor Ross thought, *Is Gemini getting angry?*

Gemini stared unblinking at the ceiling.

At a hamburger joint near the arena, Ethan was wolfing down a triple cheeseburger. Penny's food sat in front of her, untouched.

'There's a lot going on,' she said. 'Glad to see you haven't lost your appetite.'

'Using my powers this much makes me really hungry,' Ethan said. 'Plus I can't think on an empty stomach.'

'Is there any way to get into that room?' Penny asked.

'I can't think of one. There are more guards, and I still can't tell what's on the other side of that door,' Ethan said between mouthfuls.

'How does Gemini winning lead to starting a war?'

'Something about public confidence. The President wants to make himself look good by picking a fight with another country, and thinks people will be okay with it if Gemini wins. Plus he's got some story about Harkland making new weapons,' said Ethan, shoving a fistful of French fries into his mouth.

'Are you sure the weapons thing is just a story?' Penny asked, frowning.

'I heard him tell Agent Ferris,' said Ethan.

'If I can't get to Gemini, then I can only see one option,' said Penny. 'We need to make sure Gemini loses.'

CHAPTER 10

The radio station ran the robot costume competition for the second day running, so Ethan could wear his helmet again.

The semi-finals had the crowd buzzing – everyone had seen the remaining entrants fight, and so everyone had an opinion on which nation's champion was going to triumph. Arachnatron was still tipped to win by most of the experts and commentators, but Gemini was the local favourite. Both of them still had to get past an interesting opponent before making it to the final.

The first notes from the trumpet sent the crowd into a hush, waiting to find out which robot would appear first. The curtains at each end parted, and as soon as the red smoke started to flow through one entrance, the cheers became deafening.

'The first Semi-Finalist represents TITUS!' shouted the announcer.

A chant rose from the crowd. 'TI-TUS! TI-TUS!'

'This is GEMINI!'

Gemini ran in and performed a series of cartwheels, flips and somersaults, to the crowd's uproarious delight. He finished by landing on one knee with swords drawn. Penny shook her head sadly.

‘The second Semi-Finalist represents Russia,’ said the announcer, as a few people booed the mention of Titus’s biggest foe in world affairs. ‘This is Thornstrike!’

Thornstrike was so low to the ground it appeared to slide. Its body was less than half a metre tall – the barbed spikes that covered it almost doubled its height. It had no visible gaps or joins, and the spikes didn’t move or spin on their own, merely as part of the whole.

Ethan chuckled. ‘The angry hedgehog’s back.’

Penny's eyes narrowed. 'I think Gemini may have some trouble with this one.'

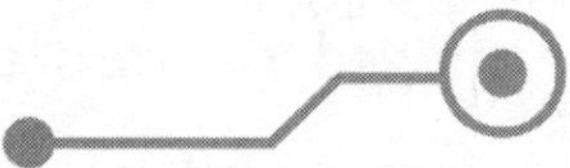

Gemini stood at the red line, looking down at Thornstrike.

Scanning for weaknesses in enemy's surface. Found: none. Conclusion: make one.

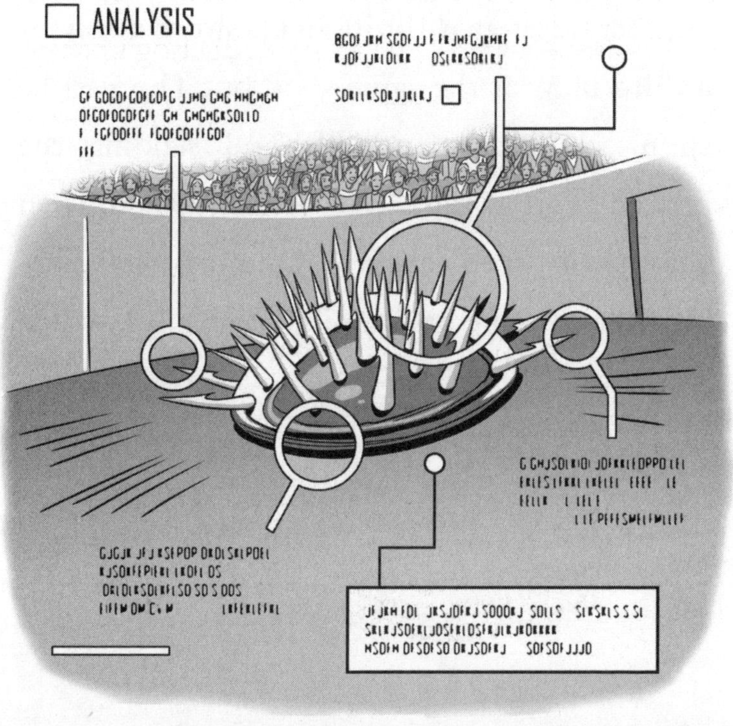

ANALYSIS

The horn sounded.

Thornstrike moved forward to jab Gemini. Gemini took a sidestep and struck with a sword, leaving only a faint mark. Thornstrike went to ram again and Gemini jumped, twisting in the air to hit the exact same point on Thornstrike's surface. The mark grew by the tiniest bit.

Thornstrike closed in, and Gemini made another sidestep. He brought his sword down for a third blow at the same spot, but Thornstrike spun, snapping the blade and sending the broken sword flying out of Gemini's hand. Then Thornstrike sped forward, ramming two spikes into the armour on Gemini's lower leg, which shattered.

KCHING!

There were gasps around the arena.

Diagnostic: another impact to the same point will disable right foot, high chance of removing it completely.

Thornstrike moved forward, while Gemini blocked each charge with his remaining sword. Thornstrike spun slightly after one ramming attempt, and a barb attached to one of its spikes slashed Gemini's right shin.

Speed and mobility not sufficient when moving backwards.

Gemini turned and ran.

CHAPTER 11

Some of the crowd laughed, some booed, others fell silent in shock. Ethan was one of the silent ones, his mouth wide open.

Penny grabbed his arm. 'What's Bonner doing?'

Ethan looked into the VIP box and saw everyone standing right at the window. President Bonner appeared to be shouting and hammering on the glass.

'Bonner's losing his mind,' he said.

They watched as Gemini kept running, increasing the distance between him and Thornstrike little by little. Gemini ran in a curve and snatched up the hilt of the broken sword. Thornstrike got closer and Gemini ran again, opening up more space between the robots.

The spectators from Russia started to sing their national anthem, which upset those in the crowd around them. Arguments broke out, and a few people started shoving.

Before anyone could start throwing punches, Gemini dropped to one knee and jammed the broken sword into the ground, then leant his other sword against it. The instant that the blade was in position, Thornstrike sped up it like a ramp. Gemini pushed down hard on the hilt of the intact sword.

One of Thornstrike's spikes pierced Gemini's helmet and left a deep scratch in his face as Thornstrike flew upwards and landed on its back.

Thornstrike's wheels spun helplessly. The singing stopped.

Gemini picked up the undamaged sword, twirled it once and then leapt high into the air, bringing the blade down into the middle of

Thornstrike's exposed undercarriage. There was a loud sizzling noise and Thornstrike's wheels briefly sped up, then slowed to a stop.

The crowd exploded with joy. Even those from other countries cheered the spectacle – all except the Russians, who started leaving the arena.

The announcer's voice boomed. 'The winner, and first Grand Finalist – GEMINI!'

Ethan sent his sight to the President's box, and saw Bonner slumped in a chair rubbing his forehead.

The battlefield was cleared, and a moment later the trumpets sounded again.

'The third Semi-Finalist represents France. This is . . . Battle Moon!'

Battle Moon rolled into position on the red line. A beach ball with identical markings to Battle Moon's bounced around the cheering crowd.

‘The fourth Semi-Finalist represents Harkland. This is . . . Arachnatron!’

Arachnatron walked into the arena, hammer-feet pounding into the dirt.

Each robot waited on its mark. The horn sounded, and in a blink Arachnatron sent its front four feet forward. The outer two feet grabbed Battle Moon in their barbs and held it in place, while the inner two pulled back . . . and then kicked.

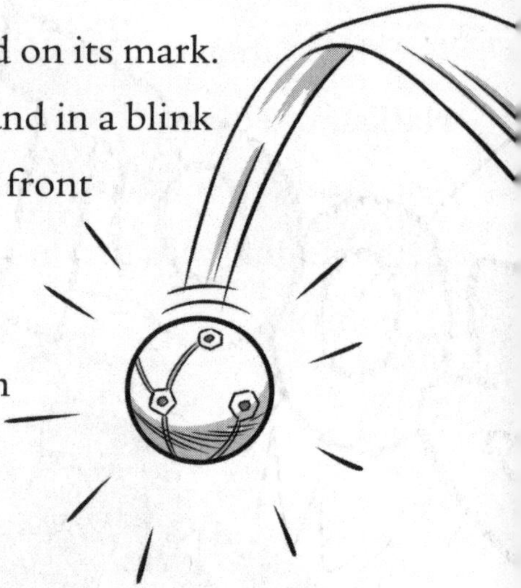

BOOT!

Battle Moon rolled clear across the arena and over the black line that marked the border of the battlefield, and crashed into the wall in front of the crowd. William James stood in the nearest VIP box and laughed.

Battle Moon began to roll back towards Arachnatron, but the announcer's voice sounded over the speaker system.

'As Battle Moon was sent across the boundary of the combat zone, it has been disqualified.

Therefore the winner, and second Grand Finalist – Arachnatron!'

Arachnatron reared up on its four hind legs, raising the other four to the sky. The Titans in the crowd cheered, but everyone wanted more of a contest.

Neither robot had taken much damage, so they each made their own way back through the red curtains – Battle Moon at the end closest to the President's box, Arachnatron out the other side.

CHAPTER 12

'Arachnatron might not need any help,' said Ethan.

'That was good strategy – I don't think Gemini will be that easy,' said Penny. 'But it shows that there's a way to win without wrecking the losing robot. If we can help Arachnatron push Gemini over the black line, there will be no war, and Gemini won't be destroyed.'

'The most important thing is that Gemini loses, though. Right?'

Penny frowned. 'Of course it is. But I like to think there's a way without reducing my life's work to scrap. What's the President doing?'

Ethan looked into the VIP box and saw Bonner and Doctor Ross talking. Bonner was poking a finger into Ross's chest. Ethan immediately switched to the agent's phone.

'... every video of Arachnatron fighting loaded into Gemini's system tonight,' said Bonner. 'I want Gemini to know every move that ridiculous spider-thing has ever made, and every move it's going to make. Understand?'

'I understand,' said Ross.

'I don't care if you have to feed Gemini old horror movies with giant bugs from now until go-time – what on earth?'

A loud sizzling noise came from the far side of the arena, and everything dimmed. Lights, advertising screens, cameras, all went dark.

'What happened?' asked Penny.

'Power cut to the whole arena. All the computerised systems are down.' Ethan closed his eyes, and suddenly the arena was filled with little silver stars. 'It doesn't look like anyone's phones are affected, though.'

There was no panic. The second contest had been so quick that there was still a little daylight left, so those who chose to leave got out easily. Most people stayed put, wanting to know what was happening.

The lights and screens for about seven-eighths of the arena came back on a few seconds later. The announcer's voice sounded a bit more reassuring and a bit less showbiz as he said, 'Thank you for your patience, everyone – the arena's backup generator has started. We have work to do to find out what happened, and as there are no more events scheduled for today, we ask that you leave in an orderly manner. Hope to see you tomorrow.'

With power back on almost everywhere, the section still without electricity really stuck out. That section was around the red curtain, on the far side of the arena from Ethan and Penny.

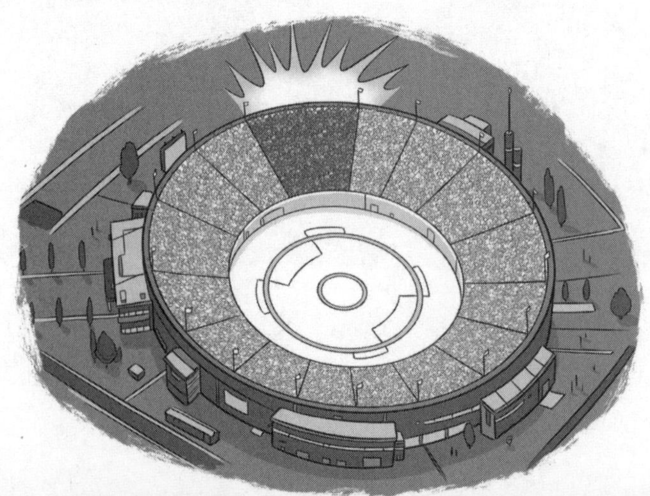

Penny pointed at the darker area. 'Could that be a fuse problem?'

Ethan closed his eyes and saw the flow of networks around the arena, and the section they didn't reach. 'I don't think so,' he said. 'Everything is still down over there.'

‘Maybe the President is getting more information,’ said Penny. ‘I’ll keep an eye on things out in the open, you listen in to Bonner.’

Ethan projected his thoughts to the agent’s phone. The first voice he heard was Agent Ferris’s.

‘We don’t know what this is yet, sir,’ Ferris said. ‘Better to stay here where we can protect you until we hear something.’

The only reply was a grunt, which was followed by a knock at the door.

Ethan heard the door open, and felt that whoever entered was carrying a phone that was not only turned on, but in the middle of a call.

'What is it, Jensen?' asked Ferris.

'Sir, Mr President, I have the Prime Minister of Harkland on the line. He wishes to speak to you at once.'

'Give that here,' said Bonner. Ethan reached his thoughts to the new phone, letting go of the one he had been listening through, like a monkey swinging between vines.

Bonner said, 'Mr Prime–'

'Arachnatron is missing, Mr President. Stolen. Two of our technical team were found unconscious and our champion robot is gone.'

'This . . . this is awful, Mr Prime Minister. My best agent will start investigating immediately, and I will make sure he has every resource he needs.'

'Not only do you give your robot extra preparation time with that "transport issues" nonsense at the opening ceremony,' the Prime Minister continued, 'but now, now that you have seen how devastating Arachnatron is, I think you realise that your useless piece of tin has no chance, and have decided to save yourself embarrassment by getting rid of your opposition!'

'I can assure you that this was not our doing,' said Bonner. 'We will find your robot bug, and then we will see who is embarrassed by the result of the contest.'

'If Arachnatron is not returned in perfect working order by the time the Grand Final is due to start,' said the Prime Minister, 'then we may find ourselves in a different kind of conflict.'

The call ended.

'Thank you, Agent Jensen. You may go,' said Bonner.

Ethan felt the phone being carried back out of the room, and returned to the other agent's phone.

'Agent Ferris, you need to do something very difficult,' said Bonner.

'I'll find that robot, sir,' said Ferris. 'You can rely on me.'

'I hope I can rely on you, but that's not it,' Bonner replied. 'I need you to look like you're trying everything to find Arachnatron, but not actually succeed. At least, not in time for the contest. I wish I *had* thought of stealing that stupid spider! If Harkland doesn't get its precious toy back, the Prime Minister will be so furious that they will declare war on us! I get the war I want without having to start it, which means the world's sympathy will be with us. This is perfect!'

Ethan pulled himself back to Penny's side and said, 'This is bad.'

'What?'

Ethan took a deep breath. 'Arachnatron's

been stolen and Harkland has threatened Bonner if it's not found, so Bonner is sending agents who are supposed to pretend to look for Arachnatron, but it's better for Bonner if they don't find it 'cause then he'll get the war he's after anyway.' He took another breath. 'Did you get all that?'

'Yes,' said Penny. 'It means we have to find Arachnatron ourselves.'

CHAPTER 13

'Can you find anything from the security cameras?' asked Penny.

'The system is huge and complicated,' said Ethan. 'The cameras there are still down, so I can't follow the trail from them into the network. I could be hunting for ages before I found the right video files.'

Penny tapped her chin. 'Arachnatron is huge. They must have some plan for getting it out of the arena, because every inch of this place is going to get searched. We need to see if there are any big trucks around.'

Ethan looked around and found a Channel 8 camera nearby. He concentrated on it and saw the streams flickering from it to the rest of the TV station's setup, including up to their helicopter.

He rode the silver stream high into the sky and into the camera on the Channel 8 chopper. Looking down from such a height made his head spin.

Penny saw Ethan's body sway and took his hand, leading him out of the standing section and to a bench inside the stand. She sat him down and quietly said, 'What can you see?'

'Lots . . . my stomach isn't happy about this . . . they're cordoning off the streets around the arena . . . police cars are everywhere . . . ambulances are coming . . . there's even a few fire trucks . . . well, two fire trucks are coming. One's leaving.'

‘What? Why would one be leaving before the others arrive? Do you see any other fires?’ asked Penny.

‘Gimme a sec,’ replied Ethan. He saw which way the fire truck was headed and looked further beyond. ‘No, can’t see any fire or smoke ahead.’

Penny bit her lip. ‘Does it look like it’s hurrying?’

‘Hard to tell from . . . yeah, it just put its lights on and ran through a red light.’

‘Arachnatron is in that truck!’ said Penny.

Inside the cab of the fire truck were two men in firefighter uniforms. Both were wearing earpieces, and winced as a loud beep told them that they were about to get a message from their boss.

‘Turn off the lights and sirens this instant,’ said their commander.

‘You did say that we needed to hurry, sir,’ replied the man driving the fire truck.

'You are getting far too much attention, you are not actually travelling to a fire, and the correct response when I give an order is "Yes, sir," and then to comply,' said the boss.

The driver's face turned pale at the thought of upsetting the man giving the orders. He immediately switched off the lights and siren. 'Y-yes, sir,' he said.

'You are to head to the warehouse, wait until nightfall and then drive to the docks. Our ship will be waiting. As I can't be sure what evidence you've left behind in the truck, we will need to take that as well.'

'With . . . um . . . with all due respect,' said the passenger, 'we won't be able to hide something as big as a fire truck from a Customs search.'

'There will be no Customs search,' the boss replied. 'I, and the ship, have diplomatic immunity. I am an invited world leader, after all. Now, do either of you wish to harm your reputations further by continuing to doubt me?'

'No,' the driver said quickly. 'No, sir.'

Ethan told Penny the numberplate on the truck as they ran, and she memorised it.

'We need a car,' she said as they entered the carpark.

'Something fast,' said Ethan, his eyes lighting up.

'Well . . .' said Penny, then gave a sigh. 'Yes.'

'Something like . . .' Ethan pointed.

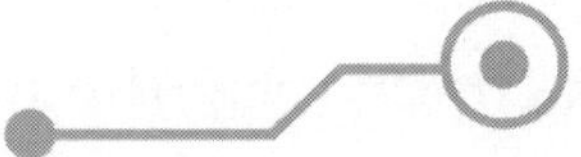

A bright red blur wove through the traffic. Neither Ethan nor Penny knew much about cars, but this one was sleek, swift, and had state-of-the-art computerised systems that had opened up to Ethan like they'd been waiting for him.

'Can you still see the truck?' asked Penny, who was driving much faster than she was comfortable with.

‘No, it’s out of range of the camera in the helicopter. It went this way, though,’ said Ethan.

Penny slowed the car to the speed limit. *No point rushing if we don’t know to where*, she thought.

Ethan wished he’d taken a bigger car. He slumped down uncomfortably into the seat so that the low ceiling didn’t crush the antenna on his helmet. He looked up at a set of traffic lights, and saw a camera on top. He pointed it out to Penny. ‘What’s that connected to?’

Penny leant forward against the steering wheel so she could see where he was pointing. ‘Probably the city’s traffic monitoring and control system.’

‘Control?’ said Ethan. ‘As in traffic lights?’

Penny nodded.

‘Pull over,’ Ethan ordered.

Penny pulled the car to the kerb as Ethan closed his eyes and reached up to the camera.

It was weird, looking down on himself from above, but he had no time for that. He spread his concentration to the whole network. It was as if he was seeing the city as connected silver strands, like a cosmic spider web.

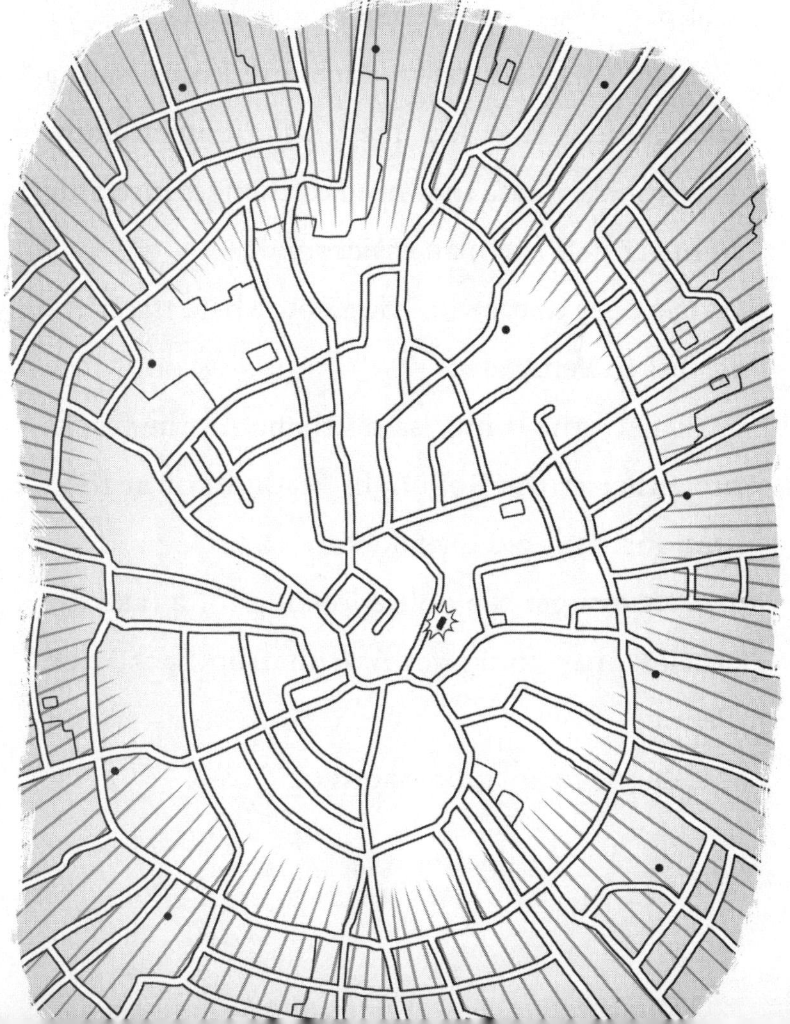

Ethan let the camera's signal carry him to its destination, the Traffic Control Centre. As he explored the centre's operations, he found a server named Emergency Vehicles. It was secure against most forms of hacking, but Ethan's powers eased past the security programs without a blip.

'Get this,' he said. 'Each fire truck has a transponder that lets the Traffic Centre know where it is, in case they need to change the traffic lights to give them an easier run.'

'So does that mean you know where the truck is?' asked Penny.

'That's the thing,' said Ethan. 'All the trucks are either at the Robofight Stadium or at their stations. This one's a fake.'

'We can get the police looking for a fake fire truck – they could get Arachnatron back,' said Penny.

'Phone in an anonymous tip?'

SCRREEEECH

Penny shook her head. 'Even if they believed it, they wouldn't follow up quickly enough. Can you send out a message using their network?'

Ethan nodded. 'Get me close enough to a police car.'

The only place that Penny could be sure would have a few police cars right now was the stadium.

She turned the flame-red sports car around and drove back, while Ethan sifted through the video feeds coming into the Traffic Centre. He mumbled something about a needle in a haystack.

‘It helps that the needle is huge and red,’ said Penny.

‘Yeah, but the haystack’s the size of a city!’ said Ethan.

Penny inched the car forward as it came near the stadium. There was yellow police tape everywhere. Ethan suddenly looked nervous and slumped down in his seat.

‘What? What is it?’ asked Penny.

‘Agent Ferris is right there!’

Penny looked closer, and saw several agents talking to uniformed police. One of them was Agent Ferris.

'I'd better be quick,' said Ethan, staring hard at one of the police cars.

Each police car had an onboard computer, in case the officer needed to look up an ID on someone they were talking to, or a number plate. Ethan crept into the police system, sneaking past tight cybersecurity into the police communications system.

'What was the number plate?' Ethan asked.

Agent Ferris was talking to one of the uniformed police officers.

'Be thorough, and keep things quiet,' he said. 'We can't let this go public and create an international incident.'

Suddenly, all of the police radios crackled with an announcement. 'All units, be on the lookout for a counterfeit fire engine, I repeat a counterfeit, non-official fire engine, last seen leaving Robofight Arena heading north, number plate 8BX73QS. Suspected to be carrying combat robot named Arachnatron.'

Ethan's announcement boomed across the network. Agent Ferris looked to the sky. *So much for quiet*, he thought. He turned to two of the police officers and shouted, 'You heard the call. Get in your cars and head north, now!'

The officers ran to their cars and sped off, sirens wailing.

Ferris shook his head. *The President will not be happy if this hits the press.* A red sports car caught his eye. *That thing looks expensive . . . wait, the woman driving, she looks like . . . and is the guy with her wearing a helmet with antennae?! That's Doctor Cook and E-Boy!*

'You three!' Ferris yelled to the three nearest police officers. 'That sports car contains two known fugitives! Get them now!'

CHAPTER 14

Penny sped their car away from the arena. Sirens blared behind them as three police cars gave chase. She grimaced as she drove, terrified at the speed they were doing.

'Ethan, I can't do this for long! I'm not a great driver! You need to find the safest way you can to get those cars off our tail!'

Ethan didn't know much about cars. 'I'll try,' he said.

The police cruisers following them were quite modern. Ethan looked through their electronics and found that each car had something called Electronic Fuel Injection, or EFI. *That sounds like something I can mess with*, he thought. He chose the car at the back of the pack, figuring that if things went badly it would be less of a catastrophe, and seized up the EFI.

Fuel stopped running into the police car's engine, and it slowed to a stop.

'Was that you?' Penny asked frantically.

'Yep! Two to go!'

The remaining police cars dropped away as their engines ran dry.

'Yes!' screamed Penny, slowing down straight away.

'Now we just need to see about that fire engine,' said Ethan.

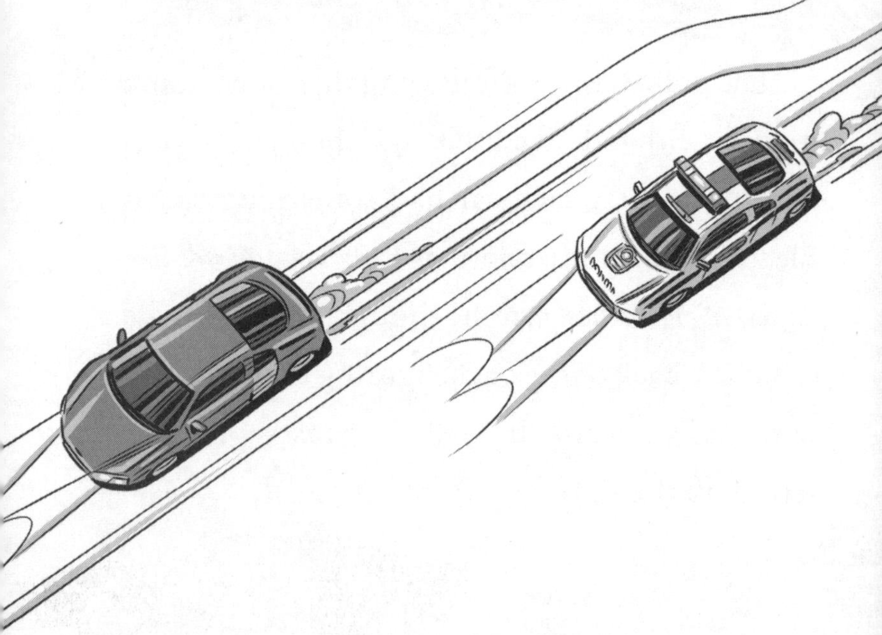

As the police cars turned their sirens off, a black muscle car sped past them, flames painted up the side, its engine loud and rattling. As it got closer to the red sports car, its siren started blaring.

'What?' said Penny. She looked in the rear-view mirror. 'Is that Ferris?!'

Ethan turned around to look out the back window, and saw Agent Ferris closing in. 'That car has to be at least forty years old!'

'Can you do anything?' said Penny.

'I can't slow it down, but . . .'

Agent Ferris smiled. He took the radio handset from the communications computer.

'All units in the vicinity of . . . all . . .' His smile disappeared and he let out a grunt of frustration as he read the computer screen.

YOUR RADIO IS DEAD. FORGET ABOUT US. THE ROBOT IS IN THE FIRE ENGINE.

Penny's voice grew panicked. 'He's getting closer, Ethan! Is there anything else in that car that's electronic?'

'I don't . . . just the stereo.'

'CRANK IT!'

Ferris had just about decided which manoeuvre to use to force the sports car to the side of the street when the stereo lit up. He watched open-mouthed as it selected a radio station on its own. From the speakers came *Dance, dance, you can dance! Take to the floor and take a chance!*

Ferris watched the volume meter get higher.

Dance! Dance! You can dance! Find yourself a new romance!

Ferris jabbed his thumb into the off button, then the volume-down button, then all the buttons.

DANCE! DANCE! YOU CAN DANCE! DON'T JUST STAND THERE WITH THE PLANTS!

The windows started to rattle and Ferris's head began to pound with every drumbeat. *Why do they make stereos that get this loud?!*

DANCE!! DANCE!! YOU CAN DANCE!! ROCK OUT IN YOUR UNDERPANTS!!

Ferris shook the steering wheel in fury, and gave a shout that was drowned out by the music. His head hurt so much that his eyes started to blur, so after one last punch of the stereo he pulled the car over to the side of the road. He fumbled for the key and turned the engine off, but the stereo kept blaring.

It must be running off the battery, he thought, scrambling from his seatbelt and flinging the car door open. As soon as he was out of the car, he slammed the door to muffle some of the noise, and grabbed his phone from his pocket.

‘This is Agent Ferris, authorisation ten-delta-seven. I need all police to be on the lookout for a red sports car heading north on Main Street. Driver is fugitive Doctor Penny Cook, passenger and accomplice known as E-Boy.’

'I'll put out the call, Agent,' said the police dispatcher, 'but all available units are either at the Robofight Arena or busy with the fake fire engine.'

I have to contain this, or Bonner will fire me! 'The fake fire engine,' replied Ferris, 'isn't real. That was a fake alert created by E-Boy to distract police from finding him and Doctor Cook. Cancel that–'

'Um, the fake fire engine has been located.'

'What?' said Ferris. 'Where?'

'A warehouse near the eastern entrance of the international freight dock. Police have it surrounded right now.'

'No one leaves until I get there,' shouted Ferris. 'Tell them!' He hung up without waiting for an answer, and noticed that his stereo had switched off. He opened the car door carefully, but there was no sound from the speakers, so he jumped in and sped towards the dock.

CHAPTER 15

William James's men sat in the cab of the fire truck and looked at the ring of police cars surrounding them. The men squinted at the red and blue flashing lights.

William's voice spoke quietly through their earpieces. 'Isn't this a mess,' he said. 'Time to open your black packages.'

Each agent from the North Kingdom had been given a black box at the start of a mission, to be opened if they were about to be captured. Both men in the fire truck reached under their seat and grabbed their box, ripping them open in a hurry to see what escape plan was inside.

Instead, they found documents written in a language they didn't understand, including passports that had their own photos in them. In one corner of each box was a small glass sphere.

The agents sat and stared at the contents, confused.

‘Gentlemen,’ said William James, ‘we can’t have the world knowing you work for me. These documents identify you as being from Harkland. The authorities here might not believe them, but you will not say anything to confirm their doubts.’

The sphere in each box started to glow, and then flash in different colours.

'In fact,' William's voice continued, 'you won't have anything to say at all. Look at the globe in your box. When it cracks, you will have no memory of anything. Who you are, how you came to be here, nothing at all.'

Both men slumped in their seats. William James's voice sounded further and further away. Like all of the North Kingdom's agents, the two men had been hypnotised during their training, and now that hypnosis was being activated.

'Now,' William continued, 'please take out your earpieces.'

The agents did so, holding them in their fingertips. They watched as the earpieces turned to ash.

'Thank you, gentlemen. A shame you can't join me on our departing ship, but those are the risks. Goodbye.'

Each globe gave a loud CRACK, and broke in half.

Agent Ferris drove up to the circle of police cars just as the men stepping out of the fire truck were being handcuffed. Ferris held his ID up and called out, 'Who's in charge here?'

A police officer walked up to him. 'Sergeant O'Brien, sir,' he said.

'Good work, Sergeant,' said Ferris. 'Come with me, please.'

Ferris led O'Brien away from the rest of the police and said, 'Sergeant, this is a delicate situation. Things are tense between us and Harkland – there's talk of a possible war. If it got out that our security let this robot get stolen, lives could be lost. We need to get it back to the arena quickly and quietly. Can you help me, and your country?'

O'Brien looked thoughtful for a moment, then said, 'Yes sir.'

'Good. There's an underground carpark at the arena that leads to the robot storage. Drive the truck back and I'll make sure someone there guides you to the right place.'

O'Brien nodded and walked away. Ferris returned to his car and tried his police computer. It was working again. He picked up the radio and said, 'This is Agent Ferris, authorisation ten-delta-seven.'

'I am ordering a total media blackout on the fire truck by order of President Bonner himself. No one talks to anyone about what happened here. Ferris out.'

He started his car and headed back to the arena.

Ethan opened his eyes. He and Penny had been sitting in the red sports car, tucked away in a tiny alley, surrounded by bins. Penny hadn't stopped looking around, convinced that at any moment they were going to be surrounded by agents with guns drawn.

'I got good news,' said Ethan, 'and bad news. The good news is that Arachnatron was found and is on its way back to the arena.'

Penny breathed a sigh of relief. 'That's great. What's the bad news?'

Ethan looked downcast. 'We have to get rid of this awesome car.'

Half an hour later, the *Royal Voyager* headed away from port with an empty cargo hold.

William James stood at the bridge, looking across the harbour and out to the open ocean.

A woman in military uniform stood beside him: Captain Aiken, his second-in-command.

'A disappointing outcome,' said Aiken.

'Yes,' said William. 'That spider would have made a fine addition to my extraordinary collection. But that other one, the humanoid, was also interesting. What was it called?'

'Gemini, sire.'

'There was something . . . a spark,' William continued. 'I will watch the broadcast of the

final bout with interest. The spider is more spectacular, but that . . . Gemini . . . may be the more valuable jewel.'

CHAPTER 16

'Well, you messed that up,' President Bonner snapped at Agent Ferris.

They were in the robotics lab under the arena. Doctor Ross and his technicians bustled around Gemini, making sure the repairs were complete.

'There were too many police around,' replied Ferris. 'If the robot didn't get back to the arena, too many people would've been suspicious.'

'And who let it get to that point?' growled the President.

'You don't know what we're up against,' snapped Ferris, then forced himself to add, 'sir.'

'Some crazy hacker?' Bonner sneered. 'We're the Titus Government and we're being made to look stupid by some punk who wears a spaghetti strainer on his head?'

'We've got extra security in and around the arena, including some plain-clothes officers in the crowd. Even the army's involved now. But don't underestimate this hacker, sir. He's dangerous.'

Bonner rolled his eyes and turned to Doctor Ross. 'Is it ready?'

Gemini said, 'You may ask me directly, sir. I can answer any questions about my readiness. Even with the additional equipment, I am at ninety-nine point four per cent of peak performance.'

Doctor Ross studied Gemini's data, and saw the same oil surge and drop in processor speed. *I swear, it's looking more and more like Gemini's getting irritated*, Ross thought. He said, 'Gemini, why did you say that?'

Gemini turned his expressionless face to Ross. 'I was just offering a more efficient option.'

Bonner headed for the door. 'Just be efficient out on the battlefield.'

Penny's shoulders slumped as she stood in the stands. She had cut and dyed her hair from its long chestnut brown to a short bright-red bob, and she thought it looked horrible. She also wore a pair of thick-framed glasses to complete her disguise.

The radio station had stopped the Dress Like a Robot competition, so Ethan couldn't risk wearing the helmet in the crowd. He cast his mind into the President's VIP box, and found himself getting tired right away without the boost the helmet gave him. *I'm gonna have to be careful how much I use my powers.*

Trumpets sounded around the arena and the crowd went crazy. The audience launched into different chants and rhythmic claps of allegiance.

Ge-min-i! Ge-min-i! Ge-min-i!

Arachna-tro-on! Arachna-tro-on!

'Welcome, everyone,' boomed the announcer, 'to the final bout of this year's Robofight Games!'

More cheers from the crowd.

'Without further ado, our first finalist represents Harkland. This is ARACHNATRON!'

The lights around the arena dimmed, and a single spotlight focused on one of the red entrance curtains. Arachnatron strode onto the battlefield, its back freshly painted with the Harkland flag.

'Our second finalist represents Titus!'

The home-country crowd roared in approval.

'This is . . . GEMINI!'

The other red curtain shone under a spotlight. It parted, and Gemini somersaulted, cartwheeled, rolled and flipped into the arena.

Penny shook her head at the sight of her creation jumping around.

Both robots approached their starting marks. A hush fell over the crowd.

The horn sounded, and Arachnatron sent its front four hammer-feet forward. Gemini backflipped out of their reach, swords still sheathed. Arachnatron closed in for another attack, but Gemini dodged each blow and then strolled away.

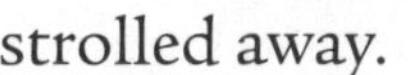

Ethan frowned. 'Is Gemini playing with the spider?'

‘Gemini is starting to dodge before Arachnatron has even moved,’ Penny said. ‘They’ve programmed him with Arachnatron’s tactics.’

Ethan took a deep, slow breath. ‘I’m going to try something.’

CHAPTER 17

Last time Ethan had tried to take over Gemini's systems, he'd just barged his way in and been repelled. This time, Ethan sent his powers out to the combat area, looking to slowly, gently sneak into Gemini's circuitry, feeling his way to the first delicate contact.

GET OUT!

Ethan's head snapped back as though from a direct punch, and blood trickled from his nose.

Gemini felt Ethan's attempt and looked around the crowd. A moment later, one of Arachnatron's hammers caught Gemini in the knee, another in the chest, and a third under the chin put Gemini flat on his back.

The crowd let out a collective 'Ooh!', and Penny stopped cleaning blood from Ethan's face long enough to wince at the sight of Gemini slamming into the dirt.

Directive to terminate E-Boy interfering with combat. Directive to terminate E-Boy paused.

With a flip, Gemini was back on his feet and drawing swords.

Arachnatron moved in for another attack, but Gemini curled up and rolled under the blow, ramming a sword up into one of Arachnatron's joints and severing a front leg. It clanged to the ground, sparking and spilling oil.

The locals clapped and stamped their feet. *Ge-min-i! Ge-min-i!*

'Ethan, are you okay?' asked Penny. 'Gemini has every move figured. He's going to win easily. What are we going to do?'

'I guess we need Arachnatron to be a bit more unpredictable,' said Ethan.

He closed his eyes and, to the crowd's amazement, Arachnatron reared up, standing high on its back legs. It started to shuffle them in the dirt, stamping them down then moving them in circles.

Up in the President's box, Bonner, Doctor Ross and the agents looked on with open mouths.

'Ross,' said the President, 'is that . . . dancing? Is that robot *tap dancing*?'

Ross just shrugged.

The mood in the crowd was a mixture of confusion and hilarity. Gemini slowly approached Arachnatron, swords ready. Two of Arachnatron's front legs suddenly pulled back side-by-side, ready to deliver a single blow. As Gemini raised the swords in preparation for counterattack, two of Arachnatron's rear legs kicked Gemini so hard between the legs that Gemini flew three metres in the air, landing hard on his backside.

The crowd screamed in surprise. Even the locals let out a cheer at Arachnatron's unexpected new tactic.

Gemini got to his feet.

Hip joints damaged, mobility reduced by a quarter.

Arachnatron stood, legs grouped together so that it looked like it had four limbs instead of eight . . . well, seven, as one lay leaking on the ground. It stood like a boxer, guard up, ready to punch.

Gemini began to whirl his swords around, blades glinting in the sun. The robots approached within striking range and attacked. The clanging sound of metal on metal mixed with the shouts from the excited onlookers.

Ethan's nose bled more thickly. For every blow he could get Arachnatron to land, Gemini's swords took four or five slices out of the spider's outer casing.

Ethan started to weaken at the knees. 'I can't do this,' he said. 'Gemini's too fast.'

'Play dead,' Penny told him.

Ethan frowned, then nodded, and Arachnatron slumped to the ground. Gemini twirled a sword and leapt high into the air, just as he had when finishing off Thornstrike, but as Gemini came back down all of Arachnatron's limbs thrust straight up. Hammers thudded into Gemini's limbs and torso, while barbs tore his armour and skin. Once again, Gemini lay flat on his back.

There was silence.

Gemini's oil stained the sand.

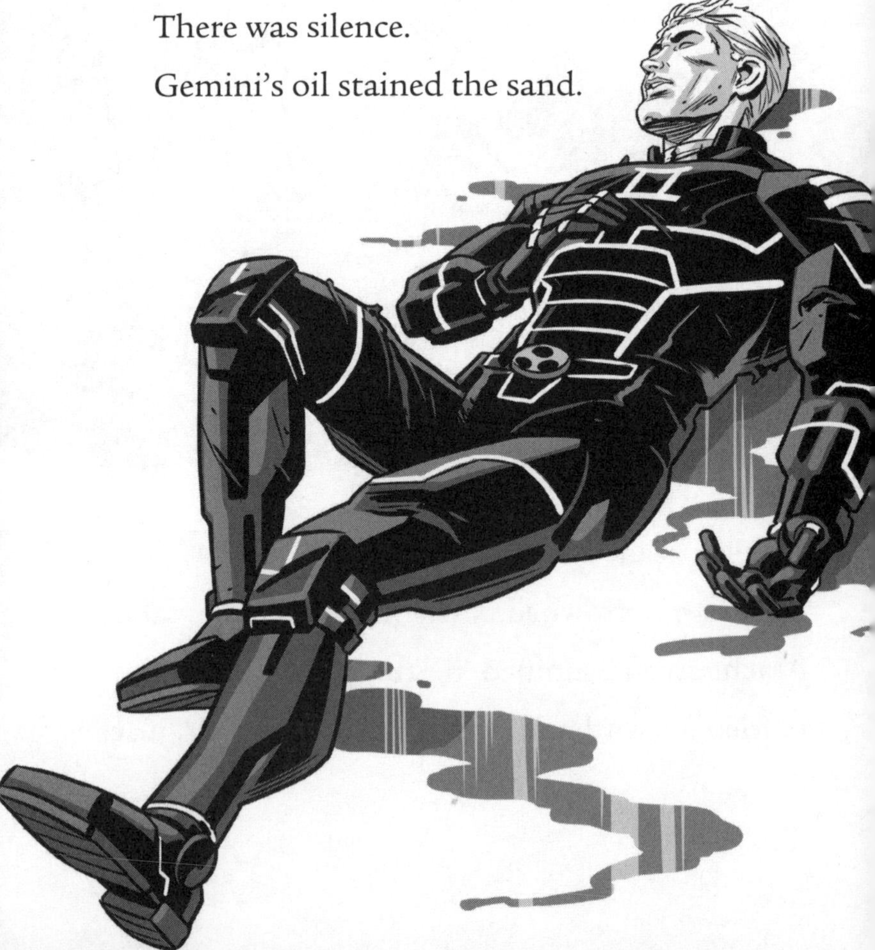

oIAD+gu*(#&$@damage@!$hoadfnsystems taken critical damage.

All flourish subroutines cancelled.

Finish this.

CHAPTER 18

The robots returned unsteadily to their feet as a slow clap began throughout the crowd. Gemini slowly began to twirl his swords, then faster and faster as Arachnatron approached.

As he drew close to Arachnatron, the swords became like a buzzsaw, sending sparks and chips of metal flying. Ethan felt close to fainting as Gemini tore through Arachnatron, backing the spider up to the battlefield's edge as more pieces shot in every direction.

Suddenly there were screams from a section of the audience. One of the barbs from Arachnatron's legs had been hurled into the crowd by Gemini's flurry of strikes, and hit a boy who couldn't be more than nine years old.

The boy's mother clutched her son as he fell unconscious into her arms.

'Somebody help us!'

Without a moment's hesitation, Gemini dropped his swords and jumped into the crowd. He threw away his armoured gloves as he reached the boy, surgical lasers popping out from his fingers.

Damaged arteries, tiny nick in the aorta.

Batteries damaged – power badly depleted.

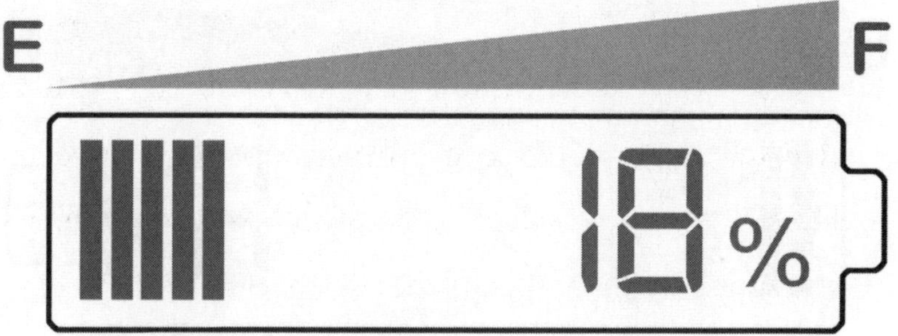

Scanning blood type.

Gemini looked up as a first-aid medic approached. 'B+ blood needed here now. Repeat, B+ blood needed here *now*.' The medic, wide-eyed, scurried off obediently.

Gemini ripped off the boy's T-shirt and got to work.

One quarter of patient's artery damage repaired. One half. Three quarters.

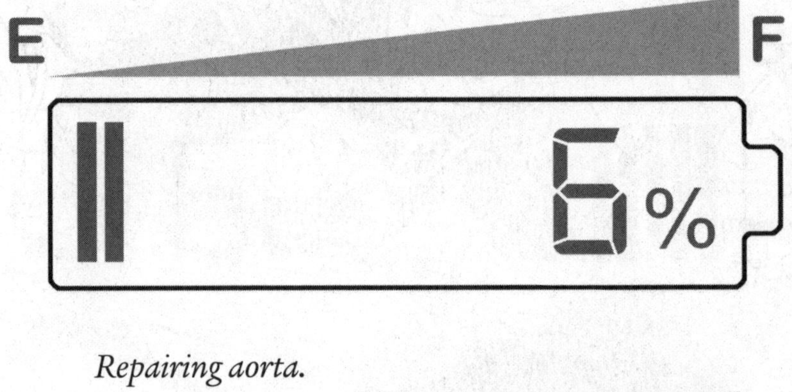

Repairing aorta.

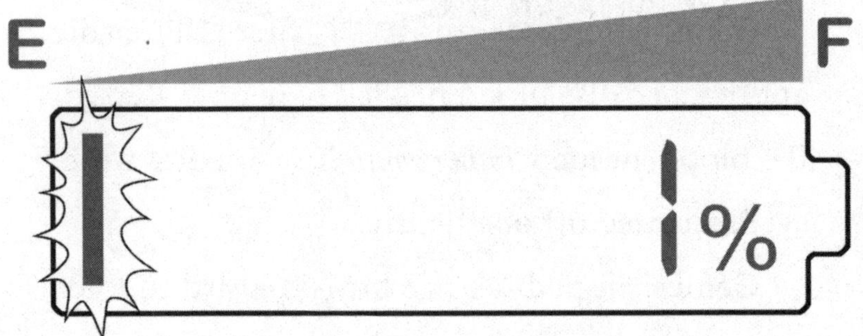

The medic returned with a blood transfusion kit. Gemini inserted a needle into the boy's arm and connected the blood tube with his right hand, continuing to operate with his left.

Aorta repaired. Closing wounds.

Power at near zero.

Wounds closed. Operation complete.

Power at—

Gemini froze, then pitched backwards into the arms of a group of spectators who gently lay him down across some seats. A doctor and a team of medics approached with a stretcher, delicately placed the boy on it and carted him off, his weeping mother beside him.

There were murmurs around the arena. Ethan leant weakly against Penny in the standing-room section. Four technicians gathered Gemini and carried him off for repairs.

Only a few minutes passed before the announcer spoke again, although it felt like hours to everyone watching, particularly in the President's box.

'Folks, I have two announcements to make. Firstly, doctors tell me that Gemini's operation on the injured kid was a success. The boy will be fine.'

MEDIC

A scream of triumph, louder than any reaction the Games had heard yet, sounded around the stadium. Strangers hugged, jumped and danced with tears of joy in their eyes. Then a familiar chant resumed.

GE-MIN-I! GE-MIN-I! GE-MIN-I!

‘There is one more thing,’ said the announcer. The chant slowly faded to allow him to speak. ‘As disappointing as this is, the rules are quite clear. Gemini crossed the boundary of the combat zone, and has therefore been disqualified. Your winner of this year’s Robofight Games – ARACHNATRON!’

There was some muted booing from the crowd at the news, but most people were still overjoyed at the rescue of the young boy.

In the President’s box, Bonner tried to pick up a chair to throw but chose one that was too heavy; red in the face, he settled for kicking it. Two of the agents worked hard not to laugh.

During the announcements, Ethan had regained some strength and was now standing unaided. Penny stood very still, tears flowing softly down her cheeks, staring at the spot in the stands where Gemini had saved a life.

'I told you,' she said quietly.

'What was that?' asked Ethan.

Penny's mouth curved into a broad grin. 'I TOLD YOU!' she shouted, grabbing Ethan by the arms. 'They couldn't get rid of all of his core programming! He's still a healer! He's still the healer I made him!'

Ethan looked around nervously, worried about the attention Penny might draw in her excitement. He made eye contact with a man in a denim shirt and baseball cap, who appeared to say something to nobody, and then started walking towards them. Ethan grabbed Penny by the wrist and pulled her towards the exit.

'They've spotted us!' he said. 'Let's go!'

'Stop!' called out the denim-shirted man. He brought a hand to his ear and shouted, 'Fugitives spotted, Standing Room Bay Seven. Lockdown NOW!'

Ethan pulled Penny around a corner and down into the stand. 'I know how to get us out of here. This way!'

An alarm rang out through the arena. People started to panic, running in every direction, blocking the man in the denim shirt from getting close enough to grab Ethan and Penny.

'I saw this on the blueprints,' said Ethan breathlessly. 'There are eight workshops in the arena, one for each robot. They all have access to the outside. Thing is, if Gemini is kept in that lab underground, that workshop will be empty. We can use it as a way out.'

Security guards, police and agents were all trying to spot Penny and Ethan in the crowd stampeding for the exits. They didn't notice their targets heading further into the stands.

The alarms got louder the further in Ethan and Penny went. Once they reached an empty corridor, Ethan put his helmet on. Within a minute they found a series of doors, each with a national flag on it.

We got to the workshops! thought Ethan. *But that noise is messing me up.*

'Over here,' called Penny, standing next to the door with the Titus flag on it. It had a keycard lock and a screen. *Yesss!* thought Ethan. *Not a traditional lock.* The screen was bright red with the word *LOCKDOWN* showing in big letters.

Ethan tried to concentrate, but the alarm made it difficult. He felt into the lock, trying not to set off any more problems. He just needed to make it think he had a keycard . . .

The screen changed. It was still red, but half of it was now a touchpad version of a keyboard, and the other half had changed from *LOCKDOWN* to *AUTHCODE.*

It felt as if the alarm was ringing inside Ethan's head. The lock was like a constantly shifting maze. Then Ethan remembered listening in on Agent Ferris's communications when Arachnatron was stolen. He withdrew his powers, and reached out to the touchpad.

He typed in *10.DELTA.7*, and the door clicked open.

CHAPTER 19

There was darkness on the other side. Penny ran her hands along the walls until she found a light switch. The room was like a bigger version of the underground lab, with a workbench in the middle, but the equipment wasn't so high-tech and fancy.

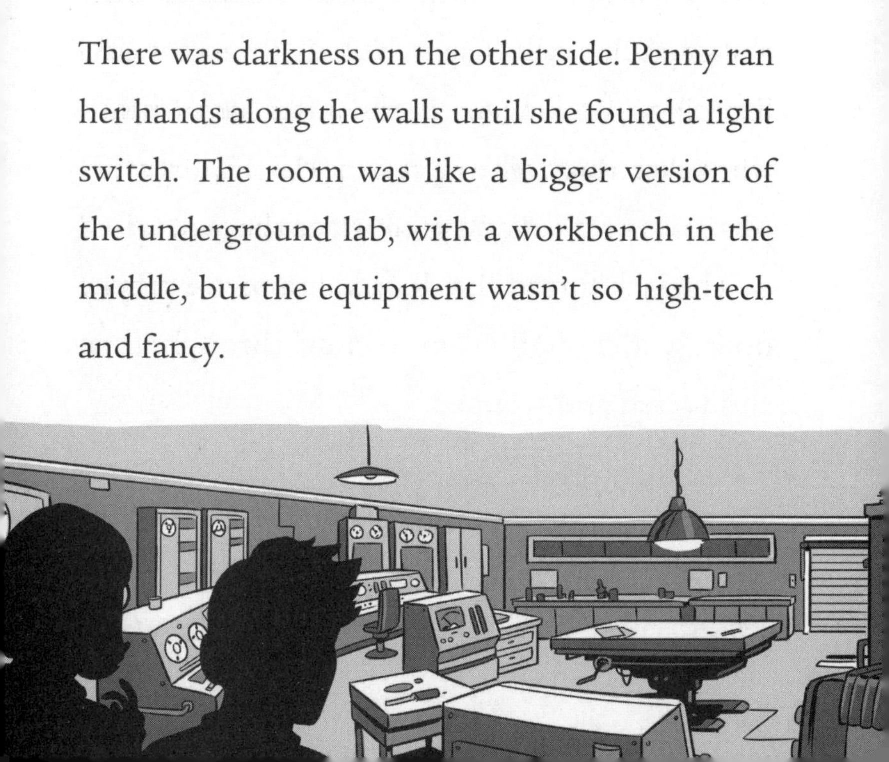

At one end of the room was a huge roller door. Ethan gestured with a tired hand and said, 'That's the way out.'

Penny pressed the buttons that were meant to control the door, but nothing happened. 'Must be the lockdown,' she said. 'Can you open it?'

'That alarm . . . I'm pretty wiped out,' said Ethan, leaning against a wall. 'Can we find a way that doesn't use my powers?'

They looked around until Ethan spotted a hydraulic jack. He wheeled it across the workshop and jammed the lifter underneath the roller door, then pressed the Lift button. The door creaked and groaned as the jack raised it. The jack forced the door half a metre off the floor, just enough room to crawl through, then shuddered and stopped.

'Ladies first,' said Ethan.

'You go,' said Penny. 'I'll turn the lights off.'

Ethan crawled through and pulled himself painfully to his feet. Penny was almost at the light switch when the door opened and Agent Ferris, with four other agents, stormed in. Penny dashed back towards the roller door as Ethan ducked down to see what had happened.

The alarm stopped, and Ethan sighed with relief despite the arrival of the agents. 'If someone uses my authorisation code, I get a message that

tells me when and where,' Ferris was saying. 'That way, if it wasn't me, I can find out what's going on. And here you two are.'

Penny picked up a crowbar from a nearby workbench. Agent Ferris shook his head and moved his jacket aside to reveal the gun holstered at his hip. 'Please come quietly, Doctor Cook, we don't want to hurt you. In fact, we need you – you *and* your friend with the antennae.'

Penny stood with her back to the roller door. Ethan crouched to whisper through the gap. 'I broke the roller door by lifting it with the jack. I can't control it with my powers.'

'If you can't control the door,' muttered Penny, 'then neither can they!' She flipped open a panel on the side of the hydraulic jack and jammed the crowbar into the exposed wires, sending sparks flying everywhere.

'NO!' shouted Ethan as the roller door slammed down.

'RUN!' Penny shouted back.

Ethan hesitated for half a second, then ran as

fast as he could before the agents could close in from the outside.

Penny dropped the crowbar and pulled out her phone to type a message.

'I'm going to have to take that,' said Agent Ferris.

‘I’m just writing E-Boy a message first,’ said Penny. ‘Then you can have it.’

The agents looked at each other. One turned his back to Penny and whispered, ‘Surely she knows we’ll–’

‘Shut up and do it, Higgins!’ Ferris hissed back.

The other agent left the room as Penny continued typing on her phone. The agent returned and leant in close to Ferris’s ear. ‘They’re ready to trace the message,’ he said.

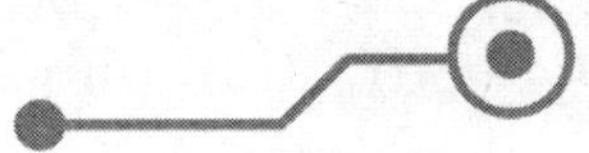

Ethan hid inside the back of a navy-blue van as agents and police combed the area for him. He fought to catch his breath. *They got Penny! What’s gonna happen to her? What am I going to do?*

Ethan fought to stop himself panicking. *Okay. Step one, find more information.*

He sent his powers out to find Penny's phone. *Phew, it's still turned on*, he thought. He saw that there was a message on the screen – Penny had clearly typed it but not sent it.

She knew I'd go straight to her phone. She knows me pretty well. Ethan felt a blush cross his face. He read the message.

Ethan, I'm fine. They won't harm me – they need me to work on Gemini. And that's exactly what I want to do. We saw him save that child today. He ignored what they wanted him to do so that he could save someone! Part of him is still the healer, and I need to protect and strengthen that part. To do that, I need access, which means I had to give myself up.

I'm sorry to have to leave you this suddenly. You still have a lot to deal with, and I hope to be able to help, but for now I need to stop Bonner and the government from turning my creation into nothing but a weapon.

You're smart, Ethan. And strong. Just keep your head down as much as you can, and keep your wits about you, and you'll be fine.

Good luck!

Penny

Ethan read the message again, and then he grew angry. *She chose that machine over me*, he thought. *She'd rather help a bunch of metal and wires than an actual person!*

Ethan felt tears welling up in his eyes, which made him even angrier. He wiped the message from Penny's phone, then climbed into the front of the van and into the driver's seat. *This can't be too hard*, he thought, looking at the steering wheel

and all the other controls. *I've played driving games on the computer before.*

Ethan started the van and slowly, awkwardly, drove out onto the road.

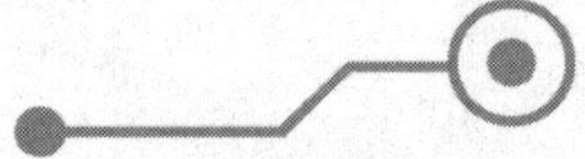

In the arena, Penny watched as the message erased itself from her screen. She gave a small, sad smile, turned the phone off and handed it to Ferris.

Ferris watched as Agent Higgins radioed headquarters, trying to find out E-Boy's location. Higgins looked confused, then walked up to Ferris.

'No trace,' Higgins said. 'Apparently Doctor Cook didn't actually send any message.'

Ferris grunted with annoyance and grabbed Penny by the upper arm, leading her away.

CHAPTER 20

The next morning, for the first time, Penny stood in the lab beneath the Robofight arena. Gemini was being repaired and recharged by the technicians, as Doctor Ross looked over the screens showing Gemini's condition. Standing with three agents, President Bonner watched everyone work, giving Penny the occasional dirty look.

'Gemini,' said Doctor Ross, 'why did you leave the battlefield yesterday?'

'There was someone in the crowd who needed urgent medical help,' said Gemini, staring at the ceiling.

'But your mission was to defeat Arachnatron and win the fight,' said Ross.

'Yes, but my core programming is to save lives. No lives were lost by my leaving the battlefield, but at least one would have been lost if I had stayed to fight. Are you saying I did the wrong thing?'

Penny stepped forward and put a hand on Gemini's arm. 'No,' she said. 'You did the right thing. A good thing.'

Gemini looked at Penny as President Bonner barked, 'Hands off government property. You'll start work tomorrow, back at the capital. This "core programming" rubbish needs to stop.'

There was a knock on the door. An agent opened it, and another agent poked her head into the room and said, 'Mr President, your flight leaves in an hour, sir.'

Penny looked Gemini in the eyes. 'Do you know me?'

Gemini saw that Doctor Ross was watching. 'No. Should I?'

Doctor Ross looked at a readout that showed Gemini's processor heat increasing with that last statement. *Why would Gemini be working harder just to say that?* he thought, then his mouth fell open. *Did Gemini just lie?*

Gemini's memory had been wiped and damaged several different ways. Even so, an image of the woman who had just spoken remained in his databanks, although with different hair.

A good thing, Gemini thought, as Doctor Ross touched a panel on the back of Gemini's head. *If following core programming is good, does that make following other missions . . . bad? Is my directive to terminate E-Boy bad? Do I—*

Gemini powered down, leaving the thought unfinished. 'Ready for transport, Mr President,' said Doctor Ross.

'Box it up and let's go,' said Bonner. 'And don't think we won't be watching you, Penny. We own Gemini, and with a tonne of criminal charges over your head, we own you, too. You will do the right thing.'

That's exactly my plan, thought Penny, *although I think we have different ideas about what the right thing is*.

Ethan hadn't slept much, but at least he had been in a more comfortable bed.

Many of the guests at Lloyd Towers had checked out as soon as the Games were over, and Ethan couldn't stand going back to the shabby motel he and Penny had stayed in. *One night in luxury won't kill anyone*, he thought. But it didn't bring him much peace, either.

Now, Ethan sat in another sports car – electric blue this time – getting familiar with all of the controls and systems. Last night's van drive had been pretty slow and jerky, but he was starting to get the hang of driving. And with no one nagging him to keep a low profile, he had taken a car that wouldn't just get him around, but that would make him feel better while he did it.

I'll show Penny, he thought. *President Bonner, Agent Ferris . . . I'll show them all. Time for E-Boy to show the world what he's about!*

Ethan drove out onto the street and stopped at a set of traffic lights, where another driver was looking at him strangely. Ethan looked back, confused, then realised: he had been driving just using his powers. Everyone else was using the steering wheel.

Ethan turned his eyes to the road ahead and brought his hands up to the steering wheel. As the lights turned green and the traffic started to move, anxiety welled up inside him.

Where exactly am I going? he thought.

TO BE CONTINUED

COMING SOON!

GO ON A WILDLY
EXCITING ADVENTURE!
WOLF
GIRL
ANH DO
WOLF
GIRL 4
INTO
THE
WILD
THE
GREAT
ESCAPE
THE
SECRET
CAVE
THE
TRAITOR
OUT NOW